John Marsh

It's All About the Money

PERCY
PUBLISHING

It's All About the Money
Copyright © 2020 John Marsh
All rights reserved.

Enquiries should be addressed to
Percy Publishing
Woodford Green,
Essex. IG8 0TF
England.
www.percy-publishing.com

1st Published January 2017

ISBN : 978-0-9571568-8-3

I am dedicating this book to all the people I love.

Also by John Marsh

Hearts of Green

Chapter 1

He stood at the counter and let the necklace dangle from his hand. It sparkled in the white lights from the glass counter making it gleam with wealth with its £6000 price tag.

Pete looked around the room to see if anyone was taking any notice of him. This was the third necklace he had had the shop assistant take out of the cabinet. The assistant that served him was an older lady, hard looking, but with a pleasant smile and a warm and comforting voice, not his sort, he would have preferred the younger girl who stood at the far end of the counter to have served him, but she just stood looking bored staring out the window at the traffic that circulated Sloane Square.

As he played with the necklace in his hand, the door buzzer rang and someone entered the shop, he turned to find it was a young blonde girl about twenty-four years old. Pete smiled to himself and watched her taking in the girl's appearance. She had nice slim legs, she wore a knee length skirt and a slim fitting blouse that showed off her figure.

As he watched her from the corner of his eye, she made her way over to the counter and stood a few feet away from him. She looked into the glass counter and he then turned to her and asked. "I wonder if you could help me?"

With a look of annoyance, she twisted her head in his direction. "I can't choose between this necklace or this one." He indicated to the counter. "For a present for my Niece. It will be her 21st birthday next week."

The girl looked into his eyes, then at the necklace in his hand. The diamonds glistened in the light and she then she smiled at him. Pete felt himself become aroused as he was swallowed up in her wide blue eyes.

"That's a nice necklace to buy a Niece." She moved a little closer and held her hand out in order for him to pass the necklace over. Pete looked into her big eyes and noticed how fresh faced she was. He passed the necklace to her well-manicured hand, taking note of the lack of a wedding ring or engagement ring. As he handed it over he brushed his hand against her soft skin.

She looked down at the necklace and then back to Pete's face; he smiled, his blue eyes glistening. "This is very nice."

"Why don't you try it on, so I can see what it looks like." He encouraged her.

The older lady behind the counter looked as bored as the girl that was watching the traffic.

"What's your name?" Pete asked as he unclasped the necklace.

"Sophie."

Pete held the necklace open and she moved forward, he put the necklace around her neck, and as he did, he took in the smell of her perfume as he moved in close to do the clasp up at the back of her neck.

He stood back and admired the look of the diamond pendant in the open neck of her blouse.

"Now that does look good. I think I will take that one." He turned to the lady behind the counter. "In fact, I will take two of those."

"Two?" The shop assistant asked.

"Yes, for being a lovely model, I will also have one for the beautiful Sophie here."

Sophie looked at him and then protested. "No, you can't do that."

"Yes, I can, you have been the perfect model and I would love for you to have it from me."

"I can't. I don't even know you." She continued her protest.

"Well, why don't you let me take you to lunch and I will introduce myself."

Sophie studied Pete's face for a few seconds. "OK, but I can't accept this necklace as a gift."

"Well, let's have lunch and we can decide later if you want to keep it or not."

Pete turned to the assistant and asked if she would gift bag both necklaces.

****

A street away on the Chelsea Bridge Road, Max Edwards walked out of Chelsea Barracks with his kit bag in his hand and a very heavy head. That was his ten years' service with The Royal Corps of Signals completed. His heavy head self-inflicted from drinking the previous night where he had celebrated the fact that he was now a civilian; something he had been dreaming of over the past year. He had completed his initial nine years that he had signed up to, and had completed an additional year, while he had completed his HNC in Electronics and Communications Engineering at the University of North London on day release.

He turned right at the barracks gate and headed for Sloane Square station in order to catch the tube to Theydon Bois, in Essex. The army had given him his last travel warrant. He was on his own now.

The journey took about fifty minutes and he had stopped in at the Bull Pub for a hair-of-the-dog pint, before he made his way along Theydon Park Road to his mum's house.

When he arrived, he let himself into the bark of a small King Charles Spaniel that was so old, it should have died a year before, but his mother was all for keeping it alive as long as possible with the aid of Lucozade.

His mother greeted him with an offer of a cup of tea and a sausage sandwich and while he tucked in, she asked him what his plans were. Max advised he was going to get a job and find somewhere to live. He had £6000 saved in the bank which should be enough to survive on for the next few months.

His mum told him that his board and rent would be £100 a week, and in the meantime, he should go and sign-on at the Job Centre until he found himself that job. Max smiled, there was never any free loading with his mum.

He carried his bag up to his room, unpacked and lay on his bed. He was twenty-eight years old, fit, slim, with dark hair and brown eyes. He stared at the ceiling and wondered what the world had in store for him.

****

Pete bought another bottle of wine and smiled at Sophie, as she sat in front of him explaining how she worked in an office for her dad, but didn't really need to go into work that much, as her dad spoilt her rotten and paid her whether she turned up or not. This caused some animosity amongst the staff, as her dad was known as a taskmaster and everyone else got the brunt of his moods. Her dad owned a property development company and she just did some basic admin work, but really it was her colleagues that did the admin work. It was her dads' way of keeping an eye on her.

Pete explained he was in the entertainment business, owned some clubs, media company, and various other businesses that 'people' run for him. Sophie seemed to be interested in the clubs, when Pete explained they were based in and around London and that he was directly involved in the Live Music and dance industry. He also mentioned that he looked after a number of the doors for other clubs.

"You sound a bit like a gangster." She smiled over another sip of wine.

"People get the wrong idea about some things, I wouldn't say gangster, I would say Entrepreneur." Pete smiled over his glass and winked.

They finished their meal and Pete walked Sophie to his Maserati that was parked on a side street. "Can I give you a lift somewhere?"

****

An hour later Pete returned to Tiffany & Co and returned one of the Necklaces for a full refund.

Chapter 2

Sophie sat in the bar, just off Kensington High Street, with two of her closest friends and showed them the necklace. They both looked at it and smiled. "Who is this guy?"

"I don't know. His name is Pete and he lives somewhere in Kent." She explained.

"What's he like, how old?" The girls seemed to ask in unison.

"I reckon he's about forty and he's quite sexy, mean looking, but in a sexy way, if you know what I mean. He has lovely sparkling eyes." Sophie smiled.

"What's your dad going to say Sophie?" Tiffany asked.

"He's not going to know." Sophie scowled.

***

Max walked out of the Job Centre and felt like shit. 'What the fuck was that about?' he asked himself. He had just been in there for over three hours and came out with nothing. He was not entitled to any unemployment benefit because he had £6000 in the bank. He was not entitled to any housing benefit as he was living at his mum's house and he was not actually homeless. He was not entitled to any support in setting up a business, as he had money in the bank. He did, however, have to come back to the job centre every two weeks to get his book signed, so that they would pay his national insurance contributions.

After everything had been explained to him, he had then asked what he would have got if he had been a foreign national who had just come into the country and not a British soldier that had just served ten years, fought in two wars and a number of conflicts, paid his taxes and saved his money?

The Asian lady with the head scarf behind the desk, had explained that if he carried on talking like that, she would call security and they would have the police come and talk to him about racist his behaviour.

Deflated and angry he jumped into his mums Citroen AX and made his way back to Theydon Bois, stopping off again at the Bull pub. He sat at one of the window tables and drank a couple of pints trying to get his head around it all. For all those years he had been paid by the Army, paid his taxes, being careful with his money and all he wanted was his job seekers allowance, which he had paid into for years and here he was with nothing.

He had now applied for over twenty jobs and had not heard a single thing. In the news it was all about the Dot Com crash and the whole IT and communications industry was in crisis. Marconi had gone bust along with a number of other high profile communication companies. This was defiantly not the time to be looking for work in the IT industry.

As he sat at his table, he noticed a women walk in who looked his way and then did a double take when she reached the bar. He looked up at her when she turned to him for a third time and smiled. She smiled back and walked over.

"Max?" She asked "Max Edwards?"

Max's clearly showed no recognition of the women.

"Max, we went to school together. I'm Judy... I was in your class."

Max looked at the women again. 'Shit' he thought, she looked a lot older than him and she had put on quite a bit of weight since he had seen her ten years ago.

"No Shit… Judy! What are you up to now….?" He asked, not really knowing what to ask.

"Do you mind if I join you? She asked, motioning to a chair on the other side of the table.

"No, of course not." Max smiled as she joined him.

"I heard you joined the Army when you left school. You still in? You look fit and that's some short haircut!" She exclaimed.

"Ha! Thanks, yes, I've just left, about a week ago. Living at my mums for a bit while I get myself sorted out." He explained.

"I'm back with my parents too, I've got a lot of shit to sort out because of a little shit called my husband." Her face looked bitter for a second, but then returned to a smile.

Max looked at her and could not believe how much she had changed since he had last seen her. He remembered a young fresh faced, shy girl and now she was quite dumpy and a rather forward, loud women. He looked around the pub and could see a few of the patrons looking on and she spoke.

"Yeah, he took me for a fool and I bloody let him. He sold our house because he said the market was about to crash and we should get out, get the cash and then buy again when the house prices dropped. Once the house was sold and the money was in the bank, he went off and left me for a slag he met in his office." She paused as if thinking about something then added. "Left me with two kids, no money and a rented house."

Max didn't know what to say. He looked at her as she finished her glass of wine and then asked her if she would like another. She nodded, and he got up and bought another beer, a large glass of white wine and a couple of packets of crisps. When he got back to the table, she asked.

"So what was it like in the Army?"

"It was fine, just like any job I suppose. I was in the Signals and worked as an Electronics Technician so spent most of my time in workshops fixing stuff."

"Did you not get to the war in the Gulf?"

"Yeah, I did, but again, I didn't really do anything. I was in the rear working in a workshop. I was not part of a battle group, so I didn't do any front-line stuff." Max smiled, his time in the Army had been great, he had not seen any action, he had spent his time in the rear with the gear and was happy with that, let the green army bastards gloat in the glory of muck and bullets. A soft bed and a well-stocked bar was his army.

As the afternoon rolled on they had more drinks together. "You know when we were at school, I really fancied you...." Judy smiled.

Max didn't know what to say. He didn't fancy Judy, she was not his type, never had been. He couldn't even imagine being with a woman like her. She was a twenty-eight-year-old, who had turned into a bitter, cold woman with nothing good to say about herself or her life and she had let herself go and blamed everyone else for her predicament.

"Would you like to have sex with me?" Judy asked outright.... "I really could do with a bit of sex and you're the first person I've seen that I know."

Max looked at her and stood up. "I'm sorry Judy; I really do need to go. I have some work to do." He apologised and started to make his way to the door.

"Max, we could do it in my car in the woods. You don't know what it is like for me. I've two kids, no money and no husband, so I don't get to go out much." She begged. "I need some fun, something." Max felt sorry for her as she looked as if she was about to sob.

"Judy," Max smiled, "It was nice to see you again, but I really must go." Max opened the pub door and stepped into the cold air. The door closed behind him.

****

Pete sat in his chair at his desk in the basement of his nightclub in Maidstone. The desk was an antique with a leather inlay, his chair was a green leather captain's style. He scanned the spreadsheet in front of him that detailed the takings of the week; from the door and the bar. It was another week where he had made over £10K in this club alone and that was just on the door takings. He was still reconciling the bar takings, and with all the other businesses including the door security and car clamping, he was likely to take around £180K this month. With staff costs of about £22K he was in for it good whack again and the best thing of all; most of it was cash, so he wasn't going to declare all of it to The Governor, who was the real boss of the business.

'The Governor' was a South London gangster done good, who moved into Kent in the mid 80's, when things were going well and now lived a high life; putting the money behind various bosses, Pete being one of them. In return for buying businesses, like this club, Pete would run it operationally and the lion's share of the money would go to The Governor with Pete taking a percentage. Pete always skimmed more off than he was entitled to, but he was sure all the other bosses did it.

He flicked back to the screen of his desktop computer, used his mouse to find a file and then clicked to open it. The image of a young girl having sex came on the screen. Her face to the camera while a man fucked her from behind. He smiled, the girl was in her early twenties, very pretty with a nice figure, and only weeks before she had shared his bed.

There was a knock on the door and he turned the monitor off. "Yes." He called out.

The door opened and a young man walked in with a bag of cash and some receipts. "This is the bar takings and stock count." The young man placed a bag of cash, book and receipts on to Pete's desk.

Pete picked up the book and looked over the numbers. "Good profits again Chris. We still getting the booze in from the ferry runs?" Pete confirmed

Chris nodded. Chris had been the bar manager for six months now, Pete had met him in the Kings Head, a pub he owned. He was a local kid with no prospects, spending his weekly giro on booze. He had been at the bar feeling sorry for himself when Pete had decided to try him out as a barman at the newly acquired club. He had been a good reliable barman, and when he caught the previous manager with his hand in the till, he promoted Chris to the role of Manager and both hadn't looked back.

"The girls still dishing out free drinks to the early sado-punters, and leading them on?"

Chis nodded, "Yes Pete, and that new girl took one of the regulars into the toilets and gave him a blow job like you suggested. Since then, he's been in every night ploughing his cash over the bar."

"Good, I gave her £50 bonus to do that. Keep an eye out on anyone else you reckon can be pulled in on that one. I'm sure she'll do it again for another £50." Pete smiled.

"OK Pete, I'll send her in to see you again when she comes in tonight." Chris said in a matter of fact kind of way and left the office.

Pete smiled to himself, Chris was doing well; kept his mouth shut and did what he was told. He had been given the opportunity to lift money from the tills but had not gone for it, which Pete respected. He liked his staff to be honest with him, and work his way, with no questions asked.

The desk phone rang and Pete pressed the speakerphone button, not liking to have the phone to his ear. "Pete." He answered.

"Pete, it's Mike." The phone answered back. "We've been working that girl you sent us. She's shot several scenes already. Do you really want us to do the gang scene with *her*? I was told she was one of your exes."

Pete smiled to himself. "Yes, I want her in the scene tonight with Harry and those big cocked blacks. As you rightly said. She is my 'ex' but she loves it."

"OK Pete, just wanted to check with you. This is all new to me."

"She *was* my girl, but not anymore. Treat her just like the rest, she now works for us and I want those films done and distributed as soon as. Franky loves her look and loves the classy bird getting fucked scenes, none of this tramp housewife shit. He only wants to see classy birds." Pete explained.

There was a pause on the phone.

"Another thing Pete, have you heard about these live sex feeds that are coming online? I think we need to take a look at it. Apparently, people log their credit card details in on a website and then get a live sex show. The credit card details are recorded and kept... it can't be right, but check it out for me will you."

"OK, no probs, I'll get back to you."

Pete looked at the phone, and smiled.

***

Max switched on the computer for the first time. He was sitting in a shed, at the bottom of his mum's garden, a shed that had taken him the last two weeks to turn from a leaking, cold out-store, to a comfortable, clean, insulated office. His mother's garden was long with the central line tube tracks running along with back, he had laid some wooden decking down and refurbished, re-roofed and extended the small wooden shed into an impressive 18ft by 10ft office building.

It contained a desk, a TV, a couple of phone lines and a kettle. His mother had been quite happy with the idea, as his job searching had come to nothing. He had now decided to go out on his own. His big idea; to build websites for people and local businesses. He had organised the installation of a broadband line and had purchased the necessary software. His six grand was now down to two grand, because of the initial expense, and now here he was, a Director of 'Your Page Web Design Ltd'. All he needed now was customers.

His own web page took a day to build, all the stuff he had learned on his HNC came into practice and with several books he had borrowed from the library, he was up and running. He had placed adverts in news agent's windows, in local papers and walked around the local towns of, Loughton, Debden, Buckhurst Hill and Chigwell putting flyers through people's doors. He'd also been on the phone cold calling specific businesses.

Success was not instant; until he spoke to a comic book shop, who had returned his call. They wanted a web page built to include an online shop. Max looked into the shop side of things, and after buying some additional software, built them a suitable site. He didn't actually make any money from it, as the monthly fee for designing and hosting came nowhere near what he had already laid out. He was still a few thousand short of his investment, but at least he had a customer, and a customer who was willing to pay him monthly, after an initial design fee. It was a start.

***

Pete walked up to the entrance of the club with Sophie on his arm. The doormen nodded at him as he arrived, and each one shook his hand with a smile as a show of respect. They made their way down the neon blue lit stairs into the Basement.

"This is where I base myself. This was my first ever club." Pete mentioned as they walked into the main area, that boasted a full length bar along the complete length of the dance floor, and a DJ in a booth positioned in the middle.

Sophie smiled as people greeted Pete as made their way to the bar. Waiting for them was a bottle of chilled Bollinger with two glasses. The club was full of people dancing and the sofa's that fringed the edges, were full of people, drinking and chatting.

Once they had reached the bar, the barmaid came over smiled and poured out the two glasses of Champagne and passed one to Sophie. Pete smiled as he looked at her in her short silver satin dress. She looked amazing, he could see people admiring her and whispering to one another.

He liked to be the guy that everyone talked about, the centre of attention. He knew that a lot of the people in the room would like to get to know him and he had the power to do what he wanted, but he liked to choose who he played with.

"So, are you going to show me your office?" Sophie asked.

"Would you like to see it? It's in the back, it's very private..." Pete smiled over his glass of Champagne.

"Private?" Sophie purred and smiled.

Pete looked at her face, then her breasts and felt his penis harden. He had not slept with Sophie yet, he had been seeing her for over a month now and wanted her to come to him. Tonight they had been out for a romantic meal and had drunk a couple of bottles of champagne. During the meal he had started to get a bit forward towards her and had touched her leg in the car; she had accepted his touch and allowed him to rub his hand up her thigh. He had not pushed it, but by the look on her face, she had been expecting it.

"If you want to see my office, it's through that door over there." He pointed to a steel door to the left of the bar.

"Come on then, show me, you, liar!" Sophie Giggled.

They made their way to the door where Pete keyed in an eight-digit security code. He pushed the metal door open and they stepped into a darkened corridor with dark blue walls and a concrete floor. They walked along to the first door and he then tapped in another eight-digit key code to gain entry to his office. The office carpet was claret red, had a deep pile and looked expensive. The mahogany desk had a green leather top and behind it stood a large red leather captain's chair. A desktop computer screen was to one side and a green lamp stood on the other. Around the walls were pictures of sports cars and exotic ladies in various degrees of dress. To one side of the room was a red leather sofa, to the right of the desk was a table with four green leather chairs around it.

"This looks nice; not what one would expect in a place like this." Sophie motioned around the room.

"This is *my* office, this is where I do my work, of course it's going to be nice." Pete said light heartedly.

"Shall we sit down?" Sophie motioned to the sofa.

They moved to the sofa and Sophie elegantly placed herself down and motioned for Pete to join her. As he sat, she turned and kissed him straight away. She slowly pulled away and smiled. "I have been wanting to do that for weeks."

Pete pulled her close again and kissed her, this time putting his hand on her leg and moving it up her inner thigh. Sophie opened her legs and allowed his hand to cup her knickers. He carried on kissing her as he moved her knickers to one side to feel her wetness. She panted in his mouth as he pushed two fingers inside her.

As he fingered her, she touched his face, then his chest and worked her hand down to the belt of his trousers, he felt her undo his belt and then his zipper pulling his penis free. She pulled away from him and moved her head into his lap, taking his penis in her warm mouth.

Pete sat back and let her work her mouth on his cock. He looked up to the ceiling above his desk to the small hidden camera and smiled. While she sucked on him, he worked his fingers in and out of her and placed his thumb on her anus. When she didn't protest, he pushed his thumb into her arse and worked his fingers in and out of her wet pussy.

As he felt himself start to cum, he pulled her head away, stood her up and walked her over to his desk. Pushed her face down on his desk and pulled her skirt up, parted her legs with his feet and placed his cock on her arse. He then slid into her wetness and pumped hard into her. She squealed as he drove. He smiled and looked at the camera. After he came, he pulled out and went and sat back on the sofa. 'Slowly, Slowly, always catches the monkey.' He thought. Sophie stayed spread-eagled on the desk as he took a sip from his Champagne with a smile on his face.

Chapter 3

'Your Page Web Design Ltd' was now going from strength to strength. Max had a number of websites he was managing and had employed a young lad, who was working from home to help him keep all the web pages up-to-date. He had a steady income and was now growing his money back to his original £6K stake. He was no longer using PC world for his supply of computers and software, as he had now found Martin, a guy in Harlow.

Martin was a strange man who ran a little computer shop on an industrial estate. He seemed to be able to get all the hardware and software that Max needed for well under the market value. Max had expanded into supplying computers, direct to his customers, and Martin was doing all the repairs when an enquiry came in. Max got a good mark-up, as Martin seemed to do everything on the cheap.

A few days previous, Martin had obscurely asked him if he minded or had any objection against sex movies; he had been told of some guy who was making them, and was interested in building some websites. Max had no concerns at all, and had asked what type of sites he was after. Martin at the time couldn't tell him any more than that, but had set up a meeting for them that evening.

***

Max had driven over to a council estate in Harlow, where he had picked up Martin from the side of the road. Martin seemed surprised to see him pull-up in a girly small Citroen AX and after telling him the address, subsequently ribbed him for the rest of the drive, about getting a proper car.

They pulled up outside a council house in a very average street and parked the car against the kerb. Martin led them to number 15, which was one of identical looking houses along the street, and knocked on the door. A large, black guy answered and smiled when he saw that it was Martin and then ushered them both inside. They were led into the front room where they stood waiting. The room was like any other normal living room with a sofa, a couple of chairs and a TV in the corner.

Within a few minutes, a smartly dressed guy in a sports jacket, polo necked jumper and jeans walked in.

"Hi, Martin!" He went over to Martin and gave him a huge bear-hug. "So, this is the web guy?" He turned to Max and smiled broadly.

"Hi, Max Edwards." Max introduced himself. Shaking hands Max couldn't help but notice that Mike looked a lot like 'Toad' from 'Toad of Toad Hall'. He was short, squat, had no neck and bulging eyes.

"Mike Franks." The man smiled. "Has Martin told you anything about what goes on here or what I want done?"

"No." Max said. "Just do I mind sex movies and have I any problem with them." Max explained.

"Do you, and have you?" Mike asked.

"No and I've seen loads of them, not got a problem with them at all. Each to their own."

"OK. Good." Mike smiled. "I hear you're quite a dab hand with the web stuff?"

Max didn't respond, but kept smiling.

"I want you to build me a website with a live feed. Video streaming. Can you do that?" Mike asked.

"Sure, if I have the right equipment." Max said. "You would need quite a bit of bandwidth, that would cost, and a good connection." Max continued to explain.

"You tell me what you want and I will get it to you." Mike stated.

"I also need to check the law. I don't know if Porno is illegal in the UK."

"You check out what you can do and what you can't. I'll do the same. You want the job?"

"Of course. How much you paying?"

Mike looked Max up and down and then turned and said. "You tell me how much, and I'll tell you whether I'll pay it or not."

They both studied one another and then Mike smiled. "Do you want to see what we want to stream?"

Max paused a while. "Sure."

Max and Martin followed Mike upstairs into a bedroom where a lighting rig had been set up. Two guys were holding handheld cameras and on the bed was an older lady, maybe in her forties with two black men. She paid no attention to Max and Martin, as she lay on top of one of the guys while sucking off the other one.

"Now take the two of them darling." A little man in his late sixties said out loud. With that the guy that was sucked off pulled his cock from the woman's mouth and positioned himself behind her. He pushed her forward and she put her hand behind her and pulled her arse cheeks apart and then pushed his cock into her arse. She gave out a pleasurable groan.

"This is what I want - streaming online son..." Mike smiled.

Chapter 4

"Now this is the live feed from the bedroom in the house." Max explained to the men in Pete's office. "The house has been rigged up with high speed SDH phone lines and the camera's feed directly to a server in Seattle, America."

"Why America?" Pete asked.

"It's to do with the laws governing Pornography in the UK." Max explained. "Not one server in the UK would host this site. I had to rent a server in Seattle who specialise in this sort of thing."

"So," Pete interjected, "because this goes to a server in the US it's legal?"

"Sure is," Max began to explain, "because the server, where the images materialise, is *in* the US, it can be beamed *back* to the UK. Totally legal!"

"What about the money? That's not based in the US is it?" Pete asked.

"No the credit cards are processed here and can be placed in an account anywhere in the world."

"OK, so how does it work?" Pete asked with curiosity.

"Right, I'm going to log onto the site, as if I was a punter." Max tapped into the keyboard on Pete's desk and the screen showed the home page of a website. 'Iwilldoanything.com.' The initial page showed teaser pictures of half-naked girls. Details stated that it was a live feed to girls on camera, giving you the opportunity to command them as you would like. There was also a price list; £5 for 5 mins and then a scale of prices up to twenty minutes.

"Why only up to twenty minutes?" Pete asked.

"On doing research it is an industry standard, that most men will pop their load within twenty minutes of watching porn." Max explained.

Pete looked curiously at Max. "You did research on how long it takes a man to shoot his load watching porno's." Pete laughed. "Jesus man. Where did you find this guy Mike?"

The room laughed. Mike turned to Pete. "This guy is clever mate, plus, he's ex-Army."

Pete looked at Max again. "Ex-Army eh! What Regiment?"

"Royal Signals." Max answered. "Ten Years."

Pete smiled. "Well, good for me." Then turned back to the screen. "OK, how does the credit card stuff work?"

"Well, we have software attached to the website which is a secure payment, but it's not *that* secure. All the credit card details come to us as clear text and we have to process them from a terminal."

"So we get all the credit card details of the people that pay on this site?" Pete smiled.

"Yes."

"OK, and are you the one that logs and manages those details?" Pete asked.

"Yes."

"OK." Pete smiled again. "OK, let's see this working for real."

"I'll make a dummy payment with my details." Max tapped away at the keyboard. On the screen came the view of the bedroom in the house in Harlow. Laying on the bed was a blonde girl in a negligée. Pete smiled when he recognised her as his ex-girlfriend. "Good choice, Mike."

"Thought you'd like it Pete." Mike smiled. Max had no idea what they were talking about.

"So, what she has her end, is a screen out of shot, so she sees our script written up on the wall of the bedroom." Max explained. "You type in what you want her to do and she follows the instructions. For example, if I type 'show me your tits'." The room of four now crowded round Pete's desktop computer as the girl on the screen lowered her negligée to show off her full breasts.

"Now, how cool is that!" Pete smiled. "Get her to lay on her back and open her legs."

Max typed into the keyboard and they all watched the girl lay back on the bed and open her legs.

"Shit, man. No shame in the girl." Pete slapped Mike on the back. "Not what she was like when she first came in this office, hey Mike. Stuck up little tart."

Max looked at Pete not understanding the inside joke. The screen went blank. "What's happened?" Pete asked.

"Nothing, your credit has timed out, you have to put another payment in to see more." Max explained.

"How fucking cool is that!" Pete laughed out loud. "This is like an old-fashion peep show, but from the comfort of your own home." The room agreed. "Max give me those codes. We are going to have some fun with Julia for a while. You can go to the bar and have a drink. I want to have a quick word with you. Tell the bar staff I meeting you and you are to have whatever you want."

Max stood up after he had written the backdoor code for the website down on a piece of paper and left the room. Pete turned around to the three remaining men in the room. "Now let's have fun with little old Julia."

****

Max stood at the bar with the remains of a pint of Kronenbourg 1664. He was standing alone as the barman wasn't interested in passing small talk. He took the time to look around the bar, the large dance floor, the dark corners with sofa's and the two poles on the stage at the end of the room. There was a DJ booth raised in the centre. The club was empty as it was still mid-afternoon and there only seemed to be Max and the barman in.

After what seemed like half an hour, Pete walked over. Max looked Pete over, it had been Mike that had asked him to come to the club today to meet Pete. He could see from his shoulders and arms that he was a powerhouse of a man. Probably did a lot of time in the gym. Max himself, was not into all that, preferring to run and be toned than muscled, but he felt he could still hold his own in a fight if he had to.

"Well done son." Pete boomed as he walked over. "You did a good job there, cost a bit to set up, but the result is perfect. The boys are still back there having fun." Pete smiled. "You want another drink? Steve get two more beers over here." Pete called over to the barman before Max could answer. "Do you know who I am Max?"

"No." Max answered.

"So how did you get this job then?" Pete asked.

Max looked at Pete and then explained. "Mike knows my computer supplier Martin. Martin put me onto Mike and here I am."

"OK." Pete looked Max up and down. "That explains a lot…. My name is Pete Yates, and I look after some interests for my boss known as The Governor."

"The Governor?" Max asked.

"Yes, The Governor that's all he's known as. He's a self-made man, known to have his fingers in many pies and if crossed; is known to have all the fingers in your hands broken, also your arms and legs. So, don't smirk when you hear that name." Pete's face darkened. "I look after a number of his interests, the pole dancing, doors, and clamping for him. He also has other interests around the globe, which I'm not privy too. I work for him and you now work for me."

"Hang on a minute." Max complained. "I'm just contracted to do this one website. I don't work for you."

"Max, son, I'm only pulling your chain, settle down. Now that you're doing this work, I want you to do some more work for me. So, this is what's going to happen. I'm going to set you up in an office, next to mine down here. I hear you're working out of your mum's garden? Now that can't be right and also you live at your mums? So I'm going to give you a place to live above 'The Kings Head' pub on the high street."

Max stood in silence.

"So, what do you reckon? You now have business premises." Pete smiled and slapped Max on the back. "You have your own place to live and you now have a business partner." Pete raised his glass and Max did likewise. They clinked glasses and Pete stared into Max's eyes. Max looked back at Pete and wondered what the fuck had just happened, and what he was going to tell his mum.

****

Max sat at the table along with his mother, Sara his web designer and her husband, in the Theydon Balti in Theydon Bois, the best Indian Max has ever visited, and he had been to a few in his time.

He was eating his usual of Lamb Tikka Masala with mushroom rice and a Peshwari Nan. His mother was having the Salmon Tikka and Sara and her husband had gone for a Gosht and a Vindaloo. Why they had gone for a Vindaloo, Max never knew, he didn't like anything spicy, but enjoyed the mild gentle dishes.

"So what's the news Max?" Max's mum asked over a Poppadum. "This isn't a normal night out, you look like you have something to say, but can't seem to say it."

Max smiled at his mum and raised his glass of his favoured Chianti. "Well, you know that new client, we have been working with in Harlow." Max looked across at Sara.

"The one with the hooky porno stuff." Her husband interjected.

"Which you have a free pass to." Max passed back.

"Free pass, what free pass?" Sara's husband asked out loud. "What you talking about?"

Max saw Sara's face redden. "Sara helped me programme the site, and it has a back-door pass." Max winked.

"And no, there is no way you're having access to the back-door." She turned and playfully slapped her husband's arm.

Max interjected. "Well, they want me to work down in Kent with them. They've set me up an office and got me a place to live." He looked at his mother who looked over her glasses at him. "Don't worry Mum, they're paying me over £7K a month to maintain their sites...." With that he realised what he just said and looked at Sara. "And yes, I will increase your wages with that."

"Cheers pal, I should be able to retire soon and spend my time on the golf course." Sara's husband piped up. Max looked at him. He was a London black cabbie and was not one for the work ethic; getting up late and working as little hours as he could, in order to just cover the bills, suited him down to the ground. Sara had had three children with him and it was because of him, she had looked for work as a web designer working from home.

"Well, I move on Monday and I'll be based in Maidstone. Not that it will make any difference for you Sara, as you can still work from home and you can manage all the local clients. It's only about an hour or so for me to get back here if you need me."

"You sure about this Max? Do you really want to be working that closely with this new client, you don't even know them?" Max's mum asked looking a bit concerned.

"For £7k a month Mum. I'll work for anyone, and as I said, the office and accommodation is free."

****

Pete and Mike looked at the monitor on Pete's desk. The screen displayed Pete having sex with Sophie over the very same desk.

"No good to me Pete, all I can see, is you mounting her from behind. You could have at least got her tits out for the boys." Mike moaned.

"Look at the way she loves it Mike. She's easily another Julia. You'll get to play with her sooner than later." Pete smiled.

"Yeah. I'll look forward to it." Mike smiled, he found Pete an odd one. Always bringing in these rich, classy girls and then sharing them around. It was all a bit odd, but he had known Pete for a while now and it seemed to be his thing and he didn't mind, because he got to fuck some fit chicks, even if they were Pete's cast offs.

"What do you think of that new lad Max?" Pete asked, switching off the screen.

"He's a good kid, clever, respectable, likes the cash." Mike said.

"You think he would be good for us? I'm looking for a front-man and I think he could be it."

"You'll need to test him. He doesn't seem to be interested in the porn stuff, and shows no interest in getting involved with the girls. Colin the director offered him one of them on a plate and he turned her down flat. Didn't even want a bloody blow job."

"You think he's Gay?" Pete asked.

"Nah, I think he's just a bit up himself." Mike offered.

"OK. He gets here Monday. I've set the office up next door for him. It's wired and camera' d, so I can keep an eye on him. I have also given him a flat above 'The Kings Head.'"

"It's your call Pete." Mike said. Pete smiled and sat back in his chair.

Chapter 5

Max stepped out of the train onto the platform at the Maidstone East train station. The weather was warm and the sun was shining. In one hand he held a holdall containing some clothes and a wash kit, in the other he held his laptop and in his head he held a plan; when his first cleared payment hit his account, he was going to buy all new gear, computers from Martin and clothes from London.

The walk to the pub was only two minutes, as it sat above the station tunnel entrance, on the main road into Maidstone High Street. Across the road, was the main council offices for Kent and behind that, Maidstone Prison.

He walked into the bar and was greeted by Lisa, a barmaid, who it seemed was expecting him. "Ah! You must be Max." She held out her hand.

"Yes, Max, and you are?" Max asked.

"Lisa, I'm one of the hired help here. Pete told me to expect you and to show you straight up to the flat." She led the way to a door situated to the side of the bar. He followed her as she went up a flight of stairs and stopped on the landing. "There are two bedrooms, a kitchen, a living room and a bathroom with a shower and bath. Not the best décor in the world, but Pete said you can do what you want with the place."

Max glanced around and was pleasantly surprised, the place was spacious, it was warm and the decor was not too bad, not to his taste, but liveable for the time being, and the best part; it was free.

"Thanks Lisa, let me settle in and dump my gear and I'll come down and have a quick beer. Do you do food in the bar?"

"Yes we do, basic stuff, but it fills a hole." She smiled. "Chef is here until three thirty and then from six to ten every day."

"OK, great." Max said, taking in Lisa for the first time. She was about twenty-four, short, with cropped hair, and big boobs. She wore a tight jumper, but judging by the size of her, any jumper would have been tight. She was not really his sort, but she had a nice smile, and her eyes were bright and sparkly.

"I'll be down in a bit then." He smiled, she smiled back, turned and headed out the flat and back down the stairs.

****

Max sat opposite Pete in his office, contemplating the man that he now, sort of, worked for. Pete was tough looking, with big shoulders, short black hair and piercing blue eyes. His face was round, but hard with a small mouth and a prominent jaw line. He seemed to smile a lot and made a lot of his expressions with his eyes.

"So, Max, how do you like the flat? Not a bad little pad is it. Pubs always seem to have great living accommodation above them. Just the noise of the punters at night to disturb you." Pete paused and looked at Max. "You can do what you want with it, redecorate, do what you want. I own it and it's yours to use for free, for the time we work together."

"That's great Mr...." Max let the sentence fall away. He had only known people call Pete, Pete.

"Just call me Pete, Max." Pete told him. "Plus, you can run a tab up at the bar here and at 'The Kings Head'. If you don't take the piss, I sure no one will notice."

"Thanks, but I'm not that much of a drinker."

"That's fine, horses for courses." Pete smiled. "Now let me show you your office." Pete got up and Max followed him out, and they walked into the blue concrete corridor. "You, are next door. Same as mine, again do what you want with it. It has an ISDN phone line, which is itemised and will come out of the monthly invoice. The rest is free. Put whatever you want in here. You are key-coded. Tell me what code you want and it will be sorted."

Max smiled. 'So not such a *private* office, as he will know the code,' Max thought to himself.

"No, all is good Pete." Max Smiled. "Thanks for this."

"No, thank you Max. The website is doing really well. I think there's a lot more we can do together."

****

Max sat behind his new desk and looked around his new office. There were no windows and the office walls were dark blue. He decided he was going to get a large mirror to open up the space, get some good lights to brighten up the place, and paint the walls white. 'This was going to be alright,' he thought. It was a bit more substantial than the office in the shed at the bottom of the garden, though he had left it fully operational and planned to use it when he was in Essex, and Sara seemed to have everything under control and had taken to becoming his Essex Operations Director like a duck to water.

Max placed his laptop on the desk and logged straight into his share dealing account. Now that money was starting to come in, he had decided to start trading. He had watched the film 'Wall Street' while he had been in the Army and he had always fancied himself as a bit of a trader. Looking at his screen he felt ready, after doing loads of research and reviewing endless heat maps, he took his first step. Taking a deep breath and flexing his fingers, he typed in the three letter code that represented the share, the number of shares he wanted to buy and pressed return. The words uttered by 'Charlie Sheen' in 'Wall Street' rang in his ears; '*Now you own it*'. He refreshed his screen immediately, and it showed an instant £40 loss on the trade, but that was normal. The buy price was always higher than the sell price, and he also had to take into account the buying and selling fees. From that very second; he was now trading. He sat back in his chair and smiled.

***

Pete also sat behind his desk; bored. He closed the window on his computer screen, that had shown an old man being pleasured by two very young girls. He tapped on his keyboard and produced his bank account; it did nothing for him. He was rich now, richer than he could ever have imagined when he was young. Growing up in squalor on a council estate, with a piss-head, factory worker of a father and a fat, lazy slob of a mother was well in the past. He had more money than he knew what to do with, not bad for an only child that society had given up on and had given no chance of success too. His parents had married young, and were both from the same estate. Their parents had also lived locally and also seemed to have had an identical history; his grandfathers worked in the same factory as his father, and both grandmothers were also lazy, fat housewives.

He had scraped through school. His parents were not educated, so acted as no kind of guide for him. There were no friends and family that he could look up to or aspire to be. His mother had passed away when he was just nineteen-years-old. He had taken on the council flat lease and lived in the house along with his father, until his father died choking on his own vomit in bed one night. He then purchased the flat from the council, through the 'right to buy' scheme, and that had been the start of the making of him. He had released some of the equity to buy warehouse knock-offs, in order to then sell them again down the market; he had a good eye for what people wanted. After a while, he got noticed by The Governor, as the warehouse he was buying his gear from, was run by his men, and was also a well-known source of stolen goods from various activities now being resold as legitimate. Pete knew how to make money and The Governor recognised that, choosing to surround himself with people who made money. He gave Pete an offer he couldn't refuse, and as they say 'the rest is history.'

At the age of twenty, Pete had met Lorraine and she was everything to him. She was not only beautiful, she was clever. She had a good job in the City, a good family, a big house, a car, a personality, absolutely everything Pete had ever wanted in a girlfriend. He remembered the night he was working the door of a club, she frequented and that evening she had stayed behind along with the club owner's friend. They had got to talking and had hit it off straight away.

Their relationship was a whirlwind few weeks and Pete was on cloud nine. He had moved into her penthouse flat in Maidstone that overlooked the river. They had spent weekends on the boat her father owned, travelling up and down the Medway. It was the summer and the days seemed to last forever. Lorraine was perfect; sexy, friendly, warm and attentive. They drove around the Kent countryside in her convertible Mercedes SL. Nothing could've been better until the day he met her family.

On the steps of her parent's manor house, he was introduced to her mother, instantly he could feel that she hadn't taken to him, then he met her brothers, they turned on him as soon as he walked in, with their sideways looks and snidely remarks. He had arrived with a bunch of flowers for her mother, her favourite kind, and a bottle of Fleurie wine for her father. The flowers had been cast aside and the bottle of wine had not been drunk at the meal. There had been no real words said, apart from sly digs at his choice of occupation and a nose raising when explaining his plans of setting up his own company, although as yet he was not sure what he wanted to get into.

They had both left together that night, Pete had felt annoyed that he had not been clever or witty enough to fend off the onslaught. Lorraine over the next few days, had started to become cold and distant. She started not returning to the flat until late, and sometimes she would say she had to stay in the City for the night, as she had deadlines to meet. Then one evening she asked him to move out of the flat and leave the keys in the post box.

Pete didn't have much, but he did have his pride; he packed his stuff, put the keys in the post box and never looked back. He didn't rise to the situation: Fuck-em! He'd show them. He really wanted to hurt the whole family for looking down on him, at the time, but he never did. He never knew what happened to Lorraine. He knew that her parents didn't live in the big manor house anymore; as he had seen it go on the market a few years ago. He had been tempted to buy it, out of spite, but that would have brought bad karma. 'Leave the past in the past', that was his way of doing things. So he just left the whole situation to his imagination, and was happy to believe that they had come into hard times, the business had failed and they had lost the lot. Or, one of them, or all of them were dead.

He promised himself after splitting with Lorraine, that no one would ever intimidate him with money, power or status again. He would become the intimidator.

Chapter 6

Max couldn't believe the way his life was rapidly changing. He now sat in his own newly acquired red leather desk chair and stared at six computer screens that were mounted to the wall, to his right-hand side. The screens flashed red and green with banks of figures continuously changing; the charts all showing an upward trend. A further two additional screens sat on his desk, one depicting buy and sell buttons, the other, his inbox for his emails.

Life was good; the web business was making lots of money. Pete's sex site was on a standard retainer fee and he now had a number of other sites up and running; one for escorts, the other for sex toys among other things.

He had kept the adult side of the business and the mainstream web company separate. They were managed under separate Limited Companies. The mainstream business was operated out of a server based in Canary Wharf and the adult one, out of a server in Seattle. He had made Sara the Director of the mainstream company, with her husband as secretary, purely for Company's House regulations, and to cover himself so that if anyone was to do a simple search, his name would not show up on any paperwork.

He had had a contract drawn up which made him a silent partner, the original company had been dissolved and the clients had been seamlessly moved over to the new company, owned by Sara and her husband. Under the new contract they were paid a retainer for Director/ Secretary duties and given twenty-five percent of the profits after all expenses.

They now employed a sales team of three, who cold-called every business in the Yellow Pages offering the opportunity to have their own website. The internet was exploding; it was the place to do business. It was like the wild west of the 1900's; it was frontier land. Google had appeared, as had eBay, and Amazon, the dot.com sector was coined as a phrase and was now booming. The Nasdaq was a sure fire way to make money.

Max was placing money on the stock market at 8:00am when the market opened; he went off to take a shower and by the time he was dry, the stock was up an average of 5%. It was like shooting fish in a barrel. Some people would have to work all day for what he was earning in ten minutes. Sometimes, he may have to wait a few days, but the money was silly. The more he ploughed in, the bigger the return.

He had earned around £21K a year in the army, he earned that in less than two months now. Sometimes, he sadly thought that he had wasted his time doing his ten years of service and often wondered where he would have been now, but he also recalled the fun he had had. Where else would he have been paid to play with guns, parachutes, tanks and travel the world at such a young age. Life is a journey; some paths you have to just follow in order to get to the roads that are meant for you.

There was a ring from his desk phone and he could see it was the intercom. Pete had given him an additional new phone that connected to the internal network, a feature which Pete liked to utilise to its full potential.

"Hi Pete, what can I do for you?" Max asked.

"Pop in my office would you Max, I've got something I'd like to run by you." The intercom commanded.

Max pressed the silence button, made sure is office was door was locked and made his way to Pete's office next door.

He had now been based in the club for six weeks and all had been good. Pete left him alone, some of the staff would say hello as he passed through the club to get to his office, but Max was not one for socialising, he didn't care for the club scene and would rather go to the local pub, or stay at home most evenings and play on his x-box. Lisa had come up a few times, but he had gently re-buffed any of her advances. He was not in the mood for any female company. He was happy doing his own thing, the shares, the money and the web business. He enjoyed his own company; he enjoyed working.

He walked into Pete's office and was greeted by Pete sitting at his desk and a young blonde sitting on the sofa. "Hi Max, you haven't met, but this here is my squeeze Sophie."

Max turned to look at Sophie, sitting, surrounded by shopping bags from various upmarket clothes shops. She was very pretty, and judging by the way she held her head, was also very arrogant. She gave Max a flippant look, as though he was a nobody and she, the boss's girl, was so obviously a 'somebody'.

Max turned his attention to Pete. "What can I do for you, Pete?"

"I want you to have a word with Mike about the internet and can you come in tonight, as I've a meeting and I'd like you to be there." Pete sort of barked as though ordering.

"Yeah, sure I'll give Mike a call straight away. Tonight, what time and what's the meeting about?"

"Be here at 8pm and I'll talk you through it. You'll be doing me a favour Max." Pete looked at him and smiled. "We'll leave it at that for now."

"OK, sure, see you later then." Max turned to look at Sophie. "Nice to meet you Sophie."

Sophie looked at Max and ignored him; Max then looked back at Pete who smiled.

"See you later Max." Pete said, as Max turned and left the room.

***

'What an arrogant twat!' Max thought. He couldn't believe that girl had looked at him like he was a piece of shit. 'For fuck's sake, she must only be in her early twenties and she's hanging around with a goon like him, because he's got a bit of money.' Max fumed to himself.

Max picked up his phone and called Mike.

"Hey, Max. How's it going?" Mike sounded happy, a few down the pub happy.

"All good Mike, Pete asked me to call you."

"Yeah, Max, can I come a see you later. Pete wants to talk to you about the website, 'Iwilldoanything.com.'"

"Yeah, sure. Is there a problem?"

"Nah, no problem, just a proposal." Mike said happily down the phone. "There's a meeting tonight with Pete at 8pm, let me come and see you at 5pm." With that Mike hung up.

Max looked at the phone, then at his screens. He couldn't work out why they wanted a meeting, from what he was seeing, the website was making tenfold of his maintenance retainer. If anything he had sold himself short on that particular deal.

***

Pete smiled and looked at Sophie still occupying the sofa. "Now then, are you going to try some of those clothes on that we have just bought?"

"I have tried them all on, they all fit." Sophie moaned.

"Well, I would like to see them again." Pete stated. "Come on, let's have a fashion show."

Sophie looked at Pete and smiled. "I know what you want Pete, and it is not a fashion show is it." Sophie stood up and unbuttoned her shirt and pulled it off. Then she unbuttoned her jeans and pushed them down along with her knickers in one go. She turned, flicked her hair and looked back over her shoulder as she lowered herself onto her knees facing the back of the sofa.

It had only been two months, and she was now doing everything he wanted, when he wanted. He stood beside her then placed his hand on her arse sliding it between her cheeks, opening her up; he could feel she was wet. He unbuckled his trousers and knelt behind her and pushed himself into her. She squealed quietly as he drove, pushing her harder; the frame of the sofa knocked against the wall with force.

***

Back behind his desk, Max smiled, as he heard knocking against the wall. Pete was a bit of character, he thought, that girl had looked well out of his league. He was a big, thick necked thug with large arms and a mean face, she was an angelic angel, a bit up herself, but he supposed that was part of being posh-totty.

Pete had the trappings, the nice car, the house and the money. Not the sort of person Max would normally mix with, but here he was sitting in an office, which he didn't have to pay for, making money on a porno site. Who was he to judge?

Max tapped into his computer and looked at the figures that came up for 'Iwilldoanything.com.' There were three cameras' active and twelve punters all paying by the minute. What Max couldn't believe, was that when these people put in their credit card details, they came to him in plain text, it was then down to him to have someone manually put them through the system to credit the money. The site was currently making £27 a minute. £1,620 an hour and it was only two o'clock in the afternoon. The peak times were in the evenings and early hours, anywhere between 10pm and 4am, where they could have a hundred plus punters on at a time. That was £150 a minute, £9,000 and hour. The site was making around £70K a day. The girls were paid £250 for a shift of six hours and they had a total of twelve on a rota basis. Who says sex sells? Every day he smiled to himself. Even though he, himself, was not receiving this sort of money. He had thought £7K a month to manage the site was good. He should have played it a bit smarter, but he was still clearing £84K a year, which compared to his military wage, was amazing. Plus, the other parts of his business were earning him around £20K, so he was sitting pretty on over a £100K a year turnover, not too shabby.

Following a knock on the door, Mike walked into Max's office smiling. Mike was a strange little guy; all toad. Smoked a lot, drank a lot and Max never really saw him eat anything. They would always meet up at the bar, where Mike would have a beer and a cigarette in hand.

"Pete wants a chat." He stated, turned and walked out the office. Max stood and followed him.

Pete as usual, was sitting at his desk, Mike took a chair in front. Sophie was still sitting on the sofa, now dressed in a white low cut dress with a glass of what looked like a Gin and Tonic, sitting on the glass table in front of her.

"Want a drink Max?" Pete asked.

Max shook his head.

"This boy never drinks, doesn't smoke and doesn't flirt." Pete boomed and laughed. "What do you do Max?"

Max stayed silent.

"Plays on his computers and makes shed loads of money. That's what he does." Pete said to the room with no response. "Max, this site you run with the girls, it gives you access to the credit card details right?"

Max looked at Mike, then at Pete. "Yes." He nodded.

"Well, here's something for you... Can you give me those details?"

Max sat silent for a second, then stated. "That's illegal."

Pete laughed and slapped his hand on the desk. "That's illegal. Don't you just love this kid!" He looked at Mike who also laughed. "Of course it's fucking illegal."

"Yeah. It's illegal and I could get into trouble for it." Max stated.

"No, you fucking can't. And I can tell you why, you can't. One, we will scam the cards until they're blocked. Two, who is going to report that they ever visited this sort of fucking site? Eh?"

"Any one of them could." Max moaned.

"And do you really think they will? And will they want to take it to court? Don't be naïve boy, anyway, if they do, we'll worry about it then, let's just see where it ends up. If we get investigated, we just say we got hacked!" Pete paused, enjoying his own glory idea.

"I'm not sure about this." Max looked worried.

"How about this then... You give all the details to Mike here on a weekly basis. Mike will deal with it on my behalf, and you will get thirty percent of anything that we scam; cash. If we get any heat, we'll pull back and let the lawyers deal with it." Pete smiled. "Max, that's a lot of doe son, for doing fuck all."

Max looked at Mike, who just sat there beaming from ear to ear, Pete was looking at him with interest and Sophie was on the sofa sipping her drink, not taking any notice of the men or their discussion. She just sat there in her revealing dress, letting Mike ogle her.

"OK Pete, I'll give you the details, but Mike has to come in and write the details down, as I read them off. I don't want any trace back to me." Max explained. "He has to write them down as I read them off, OK? Mike has no access to the site and I will sort out a backdoor that is not traceable for data gathering."

Pete laughed. "You sneaking little fucking squirrel. What Regiment were you in again?"

"Royal Signals."

"So you really *are* a sneaky little fucking squirrel." Pete laughed again. "You are becoming more and more useful to me, as time goes on." Pete smiled and sat back in his chair. "OK, Max you can leave now. I've some other things to attend to, but I still want you back at eight o'clock, as I've someone I want you to meet."

Max stood up and looked around at Sophie again. She had not moved from her position on the Sofa and did not smile as Max left the room.

***

Pete looked at Mike. "So what do you think?"

Mike looked and smiled. "Good kid. Bit naïve. Doesn't do anything wrong. Just works, goes back to the pub, goes to his room, plays computer games, reads and goes to bed, blar blar."

"Yeah, I've heard that. Goes to Essex a couple of times a month, to have dinner with his old mum. Meets up with some housewife bird who looks after some of his internet stuff. Is she his girlfriend?" Pete asked.

"Don't know, but we have put some girls his way and he shows no interest." Mike stated.

"Definitely a gayboy." Pete said.

"Nope! Don't think so," Mike smiled, "we put guys in as well, nothing."

"So what's with him then. No one can be that clean." Pete looked across at Sophie. "What do you think Soph?"

Sophie looked across at the two men "Weirdo, if you ask me. To look that good and not have a girlfriend, and doesn't take any interest in anyone put on a plate. Has he got a cock?"

"Good point. Did he see any action in the army? Maybe he's had his cock blown off?" Pete laughed.

"Not sure, maybe I could ask him?" Mike laughed.

Pete turned to Sophie. "Maybe Sophie here could find out." Pete smiled.

"I am *not* your whore Pete! I'm not going to find out if anyone has a cock or not."

Pete turned to Mike, who raised an eyebrow. Pete's face looked like thunder, but he produced a fake smile when he turned back to Sophie.

***

Max sat in his room and ate his donner meat and chips straight from the paper wrapper. He had been for a run along the river for forty minutes and now sat with his food on his lap and a pint of beer. It was twenty past seven and he was contemplating the imminent eight o'clock meeting.

He had run through in his mind what Pete was asking for, and in fact it made total sense. They did have access to all the credit card details, but the question was, how they were going to turn it into cash; but at the end of the day, that was not his problem.

Looking at the figures on the website, 30% for scamming, would result in a lot of money. Fuck it, why not. Pete was a strange one, but he could see no real harm in what was going on. So they scammed a few sex addicts for a little bit of money; it's a big bad world. He could always turn down something if he didn't want to do it. He could also just get up and walk away from this lot, if he wanted to, after all, he was only there to run a few websites.

***

Sophie got up from the sofa and moaned at Pete as he sat at his desk. "Why do you want me to wear this dress in here Pete, you can see everything. It's so short, it hardly covers my boobs and I can't wear anything under it."

"It looks nice on you, babe, and you look nice in it." He smiled at her.

"Yes, but all your friends can see me. I can see them all looking at me, ogling me. It's horrible, Pete." Sophie carried on moaning.

"It's nice babe, I like it. I like them looking at you, wanting you, but not being able to have you. It turns me on that you turn them on."

"It makes me feel uncomfortable." Sophie moaned.

"Look babe, you are helping me out if you dress like that in this room, you're a distraction. If they are thinking of your nice titties and lovely legs, then they've not got their mind on the job in hand. They let their concentration slip, and say things they're not meant to."

Sophie sat in silence for a while and then asked. "Did you mean that about Max's cock?" She plonked herself back on the sofa.

"Babe, it is only sex. If I wanted you to distract someone, or if I could close a deal because you played a little sexy with them, would you not do it for me?"

"NO, I wouldn't." Sophie snapped.

Pete walked over and sat down beside her. He ran his hand up her thigh and turned and kissed her cheek. "Babe, there're things that are fun in life and things that aren't so much fun." He then kissed her ear. "I didn't get to where I am now, playing it straight Sophie, and if you want to stay with me, you're going to have to play your part."

***

When Max came back to Pete's office at precisely eight o'clock, Pete sat where he always did, behind his desk and sat on the sofa were two middle-aged people that Max hadn't seen before. One was a pretty blonde lady with a nice figure and large breasts, dressed in a casual brown skirt suit with a white blouse that showed some of her ample cleavage; the other was an average looking guy in a plain brown suit, who looked like a bit of a dweeb.

"Ah, here he is! Guys, this is Max." Pete introduced Max as he entered the room, both guests stood and smiled. "Max, this is Kevin and Carol Henderson."

"Hi." Max said and walked over and shook hands.

"Grab a chair, Max." Pete said.

Max pulled a chair up to the coffee table and the three of them sat looking at Pete.

"I will get straight to it Max. Kevin does some odd building work for me when I need it, and this is his lovely wife, Carol. They have a teenage son called Adam, who has formed a band called 'Yellow Snow', they played in here a few days ago and they packed the place out with the local kids." Pete paused then continued. "Carol, currently manages the band, sorts out bookings and that sort of thing, but she's not really got the time to put in, to take them forward, as she also looks after their building firm. I suggested to them, that you could take over; as band manager?"

Max looked at Pete. "Pete, I've no idea about bands or looking after a band."

"You'll learn." Pete said. "You've plenty of time on your hands and it'll give you something to do in the evenings." Pete stared at Max waiting for a response. "I'm told that all you do is sit in your room and play computer games. This will give you something more constructive to do."

"Yeah, but..." Max interjected.

"Yeah, but nothing." Pete suddenly snapped. "You get a free flat to live in, free office, and this'll give you something to do in the evening. Carol here, will show you the ropes."

Max looked at Carol, who smiled back at him, he looked across at Kevin, who was not smiling then turned back to Pete.

"Well, if you put it like that. I'll give it a go, but I can't promise anything."

"Yes, I do put it like that, and you'll do fine, it's not hard and Carol will give you a head start."

***

Pete put his foot down and the engine raced as he accelerated along the country lane, he then flicked the paddles on the steering wheel as he dropped the gears and braked heavily for a tight corner, he turned to look at Sophie, who sat quietly in the passenger seat, he smiled to himself as he could see her breasts in her low-cut dress giggling with the momentum of the car. He was on a high and enjoying life. As he accelerated hard for a long straight, he put his left hand on Sophie's knee and slid it up her thigh making her open her legs as his hand moved up. She did not look at him, she kept her eyes forward, but opened her legs to allow him access.

Pete lifted his hand back to the steering wheel as another turn came up and flicked the paddle again to change gear. "Play with yourself baby." He said as he kept his eyes on the road.

Sophie obeyed and slid her hand between her thighs and started stroking herself. Pete touched her thigh again as she opened her legs and started to pleasure herself, moaning slightly. "That's it babe, I want you to make yourself cum." He smiled, he could feel himself getting hard. He pulled her dress, so that her breast was exposed.

The journey back to his house took a further ten minutes and as they came up to the drive Sophie had a spasm of pleasure, Pete could feel his cock rock hard in his trousers. As he pulled up in the drive of the country cottage he stepped out the car and walked around to let Sophie out the passenger door. As she stepped out, he closed the door, turned her round and leant her over the warm bonnet of the car, lifted her dress and pushed his hard cock into her.

**

Max sat in his room with his laptop in front of him. He was looking at the data for 'www.Iwilldoanything.com' and the figures were astounding, he was slightly pissed off that he had miscalculated his own figures on the hosting price. Pete was raking it in on the site alone, but now he wanted to scam the punters credit cards. Max's bit of software gave him all the details of their client's credit and debit cards that used the site. He was importing them into a spreadsheet. He had information of forty card that had logged on, in the last five minutes. The average punter stayed online for the full twenty minutes, which netted £30 each which totalled £1200 in the last twenty minutes.

Max had no qualms about this, but he could just imagine the amount of trouble some of these punters were going to be in, once Pete's team had got to work on them.

He also thought through what Pete had said about the Henderson's band. What the hell did he know about running a band? What were they called? 'Yellow Snow, pissing against the wind.' if you ask me, he smiled to himself.

He had gone into the bar area after the meeting with Pete to talk further to Carol and Kevin. Carol had started out as Kevin's secretary, until she instigated an affair with him and displaced Kevin's original wife. From what Max had gathered, Kevin was a quite a bit older than Carol. He was in his early sixties, though carried it well; he had a full head of hair that was only just starting to grey, which made him look a lot younger. Carol however, was still only in her late thirties. She had purposefully and aggressively replaced the first wife, the wife who had been there from the start of the business and had stood by him through all the hard times and financial struggles, as he built the company from scratch. Carol had found Kevin's weak spot and had used her assets to her advantage, working late, being there, and understanding when his wife moaned about him not being home for the kids. She had known what she had to do and planned and implemented it perfectly. Kevin had turned up on her doorstep one Valentines evening, when the cat had been let out of the bag.

They looked after Kevin's seventeen-year-old son; Adam. Max had not asked too much about the original wife, the son's mother. Adam had a band with dreams and ambitions of stardom.

Pete had told him that he had 'seen something in them', the night they had played in his club, but Max had suspicions that the ambition came more from Carol, to get her son's band to places they needed to be.

From what he learned so far, the band were all in six-form at school, all around the seventeen-year-old age group, which was the first thing he could see as being a problem; most clubs wouldn't let them in due to their age, and he didn't cherish the thought of babysitting a bunch of school kids.

There were five in the band. The singer, a drummer, a lead guitarist, a rhythm guitarist and a bass guitarist. Adam was the head of the band and also lead guitarist, apparently he was also the one who wrote the songs and put the music together. The lead singer was the school heartthrob and the other members came from the cool side of the school social circle. This was where their initial success had come from, as they had easily got three hundred local teenagers into Pete's club and this is what had initially sparked Pete's interest.

Pete would be more than happy if they filled his club once a month, but if they could emulate this around the southeast, he could see them being a gold mine. Max saw it as a bit of a pipe dream, but for a free office and to keep the peace; Max had arranged to go and see the band at the Henderson's house the following Tuesday evening.

***

"Look come and see me at my house and we'll cut a deal." Pete spoke harshly down the phone. "I don't give a shit about what you get up to, but if I know, and my team knows and I get a kick back then we are all happy." He paused while the other person on the phone responded. "Now I'm sorry that that had to happen, but you can understand from my point of view why it happened. Now again, all I can say is, come and see me face to face at my house. If you can come one evening, we can make it a social." Pete looked up and rolled his eyes. "OK, text me some dates and we'll meet up and have a few beers." Pete then hung up.

Pete then looked up at Max, who was standing in the doorway. "Twats in from London selling drugs in the club. Scary caught one of them and gave him a good hiding; put him in bloody A&E. The poor bloke will be drinking out of a straw for a while." Pete paused. "These London gangsters have got to realise that there are the same territorial wars out here, in the country, as there are in the bloody city."

Max didn't know what to say, although he had heard about the incident. Pete's doorman and security were made up of his own henchmen. During the day, they collected debts or worked as vehicle-clampers. At night, they worked as door staff at the club, led by a bloke who everyone knew as 'Scary'. Scary was a big Polish lad that Max suspected of being bio-polar. You could never judge his mood and he would flare up over anything. He probably had the worst personality possible, to work as a level-headed doorman. He had once found a young black kid dealing cocaine in the bathroom, after a short confrontation, the black kid was beaten to a pulp in the back alley. This in-turn, had upset one of the bosses on a London firm, who now wanted appeasement.

"How you getting on with the little band Yellow Snow?"

"Better than I expected actually." Max said. "I went up to their house to see them. What a nice house they've got, it's in the middle of nowhere with a lovely long driveway." Max stopped talking when he saw Pete's eyes glaze over. "Well anyway, good kids, and the band is pretty cool. I got them a gig in a little pub near Tonbridge and they went down a storm with the punters. Kids are all a bit young, but the singer and the Rhythm Guitarist pulled some local talent, even though they were nearly ten years older."

Pete smiled.

"And because of that gig, I got a call from a place called 'The Tonbridge Forum' which seems to be a local band place in the area. They are running a 'Battle of the Bands' competition and they want to put Yellow Snow in."

"Great! Well done Max, I also want them in here again, how about setting one night a month to start, see what numbers we get. If you're doing well with them, we should get a good turnout. I'd also like to see how grateful Carol is for us helping the band along. So, when you book them in here, make sure they bring mummy and *not* daddy." Pete smiled. "I do love a grateful woman."

Chapter 7

Max sat in his office and smiled. He couldn't believe the way his world had turned around in the last eight months. He looked at his computer screen showing his bank account; £287,000 in credit and when he flicked the screens to his stocks and shares account, his original invested value of £45K had become a stock value of £120K. He had over £300K in liquid assets. He had made, in less than a year, well over ten years Army money. He had to admit to himself that some of the money had come from the credit card scamming, but shit, he was still in the arena where he was earning lots of money. He had been given £50K from the credit card scam, which was his twenty percent for just giving across the numbers.

He had spoken on several occasions to Pete about his concern for the scam and Pete had smiled at him. "The cards just get stopped. We never hear anything else, don't worry."

Sitting at his computer he was now wondering what to do. The shares were steadily rising, the internet company was ticking over and Sara and her husband had the clients under control and slowly growing the client list. Max had given her a pay rise along with a budget, in order to manage her part of the business independently. Everything was going well, so all he seemed to be doing nowadays was making phone calls for the band trying to book them gigs, and there was no point starting that until after three in the afternoon, as most clubs didn't have anyone knocking around until then.

***

Yellow Snow was performing in the club tonight, the local newspaper had run a double feature on them: *'The local band that is taking the unsigned scene by storm, now that they had signed to their new management Red Dog Promotions'* Max smiled. The full story read:

Yellow Snow will be playing at the Basement in Maidstone for the second time in as many months and the band is set to sell out. They will be supported by local band' Flat Line Theory'. Max Edwards from Red Dog Promotions stated 'The band is going from strength to strength and we have a few A & R guys in town tonight to see them.' The article finished with timings and the cost on the door of £5.

Max's phone rang. "Hey, my boy. Just read the local rag. A&R coming down, that's cool, who are they?"

"I made that up Pete to generate interest."

"Ah, OK. If they were coming down, we could've given them some VIP treatment."

"Nah, it's OK, I just made it up for the papers, a good-news story always goes down well. The local radio is also pumping stuff out this week."

"OK." Pete paused. "Maybe someone will come down, with all this noise you're making! Good job though, five hundred at a fiver each, two and half grand door money... not bad son. Is Carol coming down? I wouldn't mind seeing her...... if you know what I mean."

'Chance would be a fine thing', Max thought. She was a middle-class woman who had a lovely house and a lovely husband, why would she even contemplate messing about with a brainless thug like Pete. She was a different class altogether.

"Anyway, Max, got things to do today. Make sure tonight goes well, a good bit of press for the club will do us good." With that Pete hung up.

***

Max smiled. It was now 7:15pm and a noisy queue of teenagers stood along the street and continued around the corner, along with a few press photographers hanging around taking pictures. The doors were supposed to open at 7pm, but he was using delay tactics on purpose, to create some hype and excitement.

The bouncers ushered the kids in as their five pounds were paid. Each kid got a stamp, of a red paw print of 'Red Dog Promotions,' on the back of their hand and had their bags searched for bottles of water, alcohol and any drugs.

Max stayed at the entrance door, watching and greeting people as they entered. He had a few important people in too; two local journalists, a couple of guys from the Musicians Channel that had just started broadcasting on Sky and a few other club owners. Just before 8pm, Carol turned up, made-up to the nines, looking glamorous and wearing a smart dress suit with a white blouse; she looked about ten years younger all done-up. Max greeted her and advised that Pete wanted a chat, so she made her way to his office, escorted by a doorman.

By 8pm the club was rammed with teenagers, all drinking soft drinks. Pete's bar was going to make a fortune, as the mark-up on soft drinks was scandalous. The DJ was playing all the latest popular tracks and the kids were loving it. The support band Flatline Theory was due on at 8:15pm.

Max made his way to the back of the stage to the bands dressing rooms. Even though they had been given a dressing room each, he found them all in the one room. The guys from Flatline Theory looked nervous, as this was the biggest gig since their end-of-year Prom, even though half the kids out front, were the very same kids from that prom.

"OK lads, let's get to it." Max said and the three young guys got up and made their way out to the stage. The DJ dropped the lights and the usual announcements were made. "Welcome to stage…. 'Flatline Theory.'" There were loud cheers as the drummer introduced the first track with his 'into drumming' before the guitar kicked in and the lead singer screamed his first lyrics. The place went wild.

Max made his way out onto the dance floor where kids were bouncing around, screaming and just having a good time. Pleased with the turnout, he looked around for Pete, but couldn't see him, so made his way to his office. He knocked, then stepped in, to see Carol on the sofa with her head in Pete's lap and her blouse undone. Max quickly turned around and left and went back to the bar.

Max didn't know what is was about Pete but he sure knew how to charm the ladies. Max ordered a beer and stood and watched the band.

***

The warm-up band did a thirty-minute set, followed by a twenty-minute break before Yellow Snow would take to the stage. Once 'Flatline Theory' had finished the DJ kicked in and five minutes before Yellow Snow was due on set, he announced their imminent arrival on stage.

The whole placed surged forward to be closer to the front, you would've thought they were rock legends already, the way the kids acted. They screamed at each band member as they took their place one by one on the stage, the singer being the last on and taking the biggest applause.

Following the planned initial dramatic pause, Yellow Snow were into their set with a guitar rift, drums and then vocals. The crowded room went mental; the buzz was amazing.

Max received a tap on the shoulder from one of the Bar Maids "Pete wants to see you." Max nodded and made his way back over to the office. He knocked on Pete's door again, waited and then stepped in. Pete was back at his desk.

"Hi, Max." Pete smiled. "She knows how to suck cock that one, Mike and I knew she would."

Max stayed quiet.

"So, Carol and I have made a deal, we do good for the band, she sucks my cock. We get her boy's band to London, I get to bang her, and if we get them signed! Well, she'll do what I want for the weekend." Pete licked his lips. "So, make sure you get that band signed Max!"

Max studied Pete, was he just a sex fiend?

"London's sorted, Pete. I've a booking for them in Camden in a months' time, they're supporting one of the bigger bands. The club has a pay-to-play deal. All they need is fifteen people, who pay to see them and they get whatever money that comes in after. Basically, the club gets £45 for every band that plays, and the bar."

"Well, fuck me Max, do they *know* they are playing London yet?" Pete asked.

"No, I was leaving it until after tonight to tell them, when they are on a nice high."

"Can't wait for the little fat one to tell his mother. She is a fit girl for her age with a nice pair of tits. Looking forward to telling her." Pete smiled.

"What about Sophie?"

"Fuck her, she hates this place, she's at her mum and dads watching telly. She thinks life's about spending money and doing fuck all else." Pete snarled. "I'm nearly done with her now anyway. I get bored once I've had them in every position, and especially when they just do as they're told, they're just fucking boring after a while. Don't ever get involved with easy women Max, find one that makes you work for her affection. It may be a ball-breaker, but it's better in the long run."

'What's he talking about, he fucks about with all the girls in the club, picks up airheads, films them, then shows his mates, shares them around, puts them on the web in porn films and now he says he just wants a woman that doesn't put up with his shit and would turn him down.' Max thought, but said. "You *are* having a laugh Pete, if a woman turns you down, you cause all sorts of problems for her."

Pete smiled again. "I wouldn't if they just turned round and told me to fuck off."

"So what did Carol do?" Max asked.

"She came down here all dolled-up, had a glass of wine and when I told her what I wanted, she said she had been expecting it, so straight away, she undid her top and, well, you saw the rest! Do you think I want that, from a nice, respectable lady?"

"But you took it?"

"She ain't a nice, respectable lady. So of course I did and I made sure she swallowed."

"Pete, there's something seriously wrong with you." Max smiled. Pete didn't smile to start with then his face broke. "Fuck it Max, I like you. You are like no-one I have ever met before." Pete stood up. "Get out there, sort the band out and let's get rich. Join me for a drink at the bar after the gig. We've not shared a beer since we've met."

***

The gig finished just after 10pm and all the kids were out of the venue by 11pm. There had been no trouble as such; a few of the kids had been caught smoking weed in the toilets which had been confiscated. Pete surprisingly, was personally very anti-drugs, never took them, never tried them and never encouraged the use of them, unless it was in his favour. He didn't smoke and rarely drank and if he did, it would be an odd glass of wine, but mainly his poison was plain old tonic water.

Once the club was clear, Pete and Max counted the money. There was £2,800 taken on the door, meaning the club went over capacity by sixty. Pete smiled, looking at all the cash laid out on his desk. "No fucker will know and if some inspector comes down I have three options; give him a girl to play with, pay him off or kick his fucking head in." Pete laughed. "Most of these weasly little shits go for a fuck about with one of the girls, some go for the girl and cash, very few opt for a kick in!" Peter laughed. "They know we can find out where they live, it's not worth them messing us about and because the police are so effin' slow at doing anything, if they bloody do anything at all, that it's not worth the aggravation." Pete laughed out loud. "I've borrowed a girl's phone before, sent a direct message to someone, telling them I'm going to do them over and what did the coppers do? Fuck all, because the girl said her phone had been stolen."

Max just looked at Pete. He knew the coppers were lazy little shits. The only thing they were good at was fining people for speeding, using speed traps and picking on kids drinking alcopops on a Friday and Saturday night. His mum had had her car stereo nicked once and all they had done was issue her with a police reference number for her insurance company. Case closed.

"Now then, fancy joining me for that drink?" Pete asked.

"Let me just put this cash in the safe and I'll be there." Max said, pulling a cloth bag out of this pocket.

The safe was in Max's office, it was a combination style safe that he had had fixed to the floor neatly underneath his desk. He tapped in his six-digit combination and opened the door. Already in the safe was a fair few bundles of cash, he was not banking any of the music money as there was no need to. He was also not going to declare the money to the tax man; not after his interview at the dole office. He was going to take his ten years' worth of tax back his own way, if they weren't going to give him sod-all for fighting for his country.

He returned to the bar to find Pete sitting on a stool entertaining two of the barmaids. The young barman, Chris was clearing up behind the bar and they seemed to be enjoying a joke.

"Here he is! Come over here Max and let's celebrate the best night we've had at this club since I took over. This music thing is the nuts and this under-eighteen-thing is bloody genius." Pete raised his glass of tonic water. "What you drinking?"

"I'll have a lager; thanks Pete."

"Larger for Max, please Chris."

"I don't think you know these two stunners do you? This is Suzy and this is Debbie, they are both new here. I have decided to have the girls working Thursdays, Pole Dancing night and also working as hosts and bar staff. They're really doing well, aren't you girls, entries and takings have gone up." Both girls giggled and Pete put his hand around Debbie's waist. She must have been all of nineteen with long dark hair. Suzy was blonde and looked just as young, and as she moved a bit closer to Max she said.

"I don't know why they call this the basement." Suzy said to Max. "This is the biggest basement, I've ever been in. It's massive." Pete rolled his eyes, but Max could see that this girl was being serious and was somewhat perplexed about the name.

"Have you ever been in a factory basement Suzy?"

"No." She said with interest.

"They are as big as this and they are also called basements. The term basement is not restricted to houses." Max smiled, not wanting to belittle her.

"Really? I didn't know that." Suzy smiled and touched Max's arm. Max inadvertently pulled away. "What's up Max, don't you like me?" Suzy's smiled dropped from her face.

"Of course I do, what's not to like." Max started to explain. "I just don't like being touched. It is a thing I have, like some people don't like spiders, I don't like being touched by strangers."

"Oh." Suzy giggled. "How do I not become a stranger?" Suzy seductively bit her lip.

Pete smiled and watched for Max's reaction as he slid his hand down Debbie's back and onto her arse.

Max looked at Suzy, glanced at Pete and Debbie and back to Suzy. She was a nice looking girl with a lovely figure, but he was just not into this wham-bam sex. He was not into 'sex for the sake of sex' since his last relationship, he didn't have any interest at the moment in any girls; especially easy girls that would sleep with anyone and anything.

"Hey guys, you know what, I'm going to shoot now, I'm a bit tired. Thanks for the beer Pete." Max said as he stood up. Pete smiled. "OK Max. See you tomorrow. Good times." And raised his glass once more.

"Ladies... it was nice to meet you both." Max left the club and Pete turned to the two girls. "Well then you two, it looks like you're just left with me to party with."

Chapter 8

Max sat on his bed with tears in his eyes. His mind raced back to his time in Berlin with Miranda. He remembered the weekend so well. She had flown in from the UK and he had driven up from Herford, where he was based with the 4ADSR division. He had booked a romantic four-star Hotel on the Western side; the East German wall had been down since 1989 but the good Hotels were still in the west.

He had checked-in early and then had waited a few hours before going to the airport to await Miranda's arrival.

He fondly remembered watching her as she bounced into the arrivals lounge in her usual hippie dippy don't-give-a-fuck fashion. She wore her usual bohemian flowery skirt, a flouncy hat on her head and a loose blouse with no bra, and as she bounced so did her breasts. Max loved her and had done, since he had met her in six-form college at the tender age of sixteen.

As she came through the gate, she bounced up to him like Tigger dropping her extra-large suede bag, she put her arms around him and kissed him. "I've missed you." She said and then kissed him again. Max kissed her back and then they walked out of the airport hand in hand, to the car park.

"Hey… Max, nice car!" She said as she got into the Mercedes.

"It's a rental for the week." Max said.

"Cool. I like that back seat. Nice size." Miranda giggled as she spoke.

Max looked strangely at her 'that was a bit of a weird thing to say' he thought, but let it go as she seemed overly excited. They were both nineteen now and had not seen each other for six months. On leaving sixth-form, Miranda had gone on to University, where Max had chosen to join the Army.

"Come on then Max, where we going?" Miranda asked excitedly.

Max started the car and put it into gear.

"I've booked a posh hotel, so let's drop your stuff off and grab something to eat."

"Ooh! fancy pants!" Amanda smiled and wiggled in her seat.

***

Max watched himself in the mirror as he held onto Miranda's hips and drove his penis hard into her. She moved her hands back and pulled her arse cheeks apart. "Finger my arse Max. I want you to finger my arse." Max felt himself swell harder as he lowered his thumb to her. He pressed his thumb against her sphincter and he felt her accept it as she pushed back. She sighed as his thumb slid into her arse up to his second knuckle. She pushed back on him more vigorously, her hand slipping between her legs as she played with herself. "Do you want to fuck my arse Max?" She panted. "I want you to fuck my arse." Max pulled out, he didn't question it. He had never done this to her before, with any girl, he had seen it in films and had heard the lads talk about. He pulled his raging cock out of her and placed it on her arse and slowly pushed in. Miranda pushed back accepting it to the hilt. "Now cum in my arse baby."

Max pumped for a couple more minutes before exploding in her. He held her for a while, then pulled out and sat back. "Baby that was nice." Miranda panted as she also lay back next to him.

After a couple of minutes of silence, Miranda turned and asked. "What's up Max, didn't you like that?"

"Yeah of course, but we've never done that before, and you did it like it was normal."

"It is normal, my roommate told me. She says guys love it and it's an easy way for her to cum. So I tried it and I liked it."

"OK…" Max said and closed his eyes and went to sleep.

***

"The Germans love their meat and their sauerkraut. They also like their beer and wines."

"Yeah, my mum likes Hock and that Liebfraumilch wine from the supermarket." Miranda chirped.

"They have better wines than that here." Max tried not to laugh.

"My mum gets it from the Supermarket for under two quid for a big bottle. Really nice it is too." She added.

"Let me choose the wine and the food." Max suggested. Miranda looked up, closed her menu and touched his leg and smiled. "It's nice seeing you again Max, I did miss you." Max smiled and then noticed her eyes drift to two lads who had just walked into the bar area of the Hotel.

Max turned to see two local lads both aged around twenty. He could also see Miranda's eyes still on them, as she smiled and they looked over and smiled back. Max ignored it and ordered the food. When the waiter came over; he used his best German, which just ended up being English by the end of the order.

As the meal arrived, they talked of back home, of school mates, who was in touch with whom, who was not, who had got a job, who was dating who and who had split up. The usual childish gossip of teenagers. All the time he could see that Miranda's eyes drifted to the two guys in the bar.

Miranda recalled everything that had happened with her in the last six months; her mum and dad were still arguing, her younger sister had moved out and was living with a tyre-fitter. Her university courses were going well, she was now studying media and PR and hoped to get a job with one of the big London or New York firms when she'd finished.

He told her about his time in the Army, the boredom, the bullying and how some guy he knew from his unit, beat and shot their Staff Sergeant half to death because he had been picking on him. He also told her how he couldn't wait to leave and get back to normality, but he had signed-up for nine years.

"That's a long time babe."

After the meal they sat in silence for a while and then Miranda asked.

"Shall we have a drink at the bar?" She smiled and rubbed Max's leg.

"No, let's go back to the room and get naked." Max said.

"No babe, let's go to the bar and have a drink, I've come all this way, it would be nice to meet some locals." She smiled as she led him to the bar and straight towards one of the young lads she had been watching throughout the meal.

"Hi, what's your name?" She asked, before Max could even ask her what drink she wanted.

"Ralf and this is my friend Hanz." The young German lad smiled and introduced his friend. "You are English Ja?"

"Yes." Miranda giggled. "I am Miranda and this is my friend Max."

"Hi Miranda." Ralf kissed her hand, followed by Hanz. "Shall we take a seat in a booth and talk?"

"Yes, I would like that." Miranda said and was led to a booth. Max waited for the barman and order a bottle of wine and four glasses. When he arrived, he found Miranda sitting between the two German lads giggling at some joke, Max had not been privy to.

"You have a very pretty girlfriend Max, very funny and very nice." Ralf laughed out loud. Max didn't know if the guy was being condescending or whether it was just the language barrier.

As the evening went on, the German lads bought more wine and Miranda started to get comfortable, putting her arms around the two of them. Max sat and watched, he was not enjoying himself. Miranda was getting more and more tipsy and more and more touchy; they talked about the local clubs, bands, TV, books, the guys were students like Miranda and their world was alien to him. The lads now started to get more touchy-feely with Miranda and in Max's mind boundaries were starting to get crossed. Each lad now had a hand on her leg and she precipitated.

Max was becoming bored and started not to pay attention to the three of them, when Miranda suddenly out of the blue suggested. "Shall we get a couple more bottles of wine and go up to the room?"

The Ralf and Hanz smiled and both said "Ja!" in unison. Max spoke up and said "Why?"

"So we can have a party Max. I want to party with Ralf and Hanz."

"What's wrong with having a party here?" Max asked.

"No, Max, I want a real party." Max did nothing and sat confused. Miranda leant over the table and whispered. "Max. I want Ralf and Hanz to fuck me."

Max sat back in his chair. "What?"

"You can stay here if you want, but I want to have a party with these guys, you can either join in or wait here."

Max looked at her as she stood up, she was tipsy yes, but far from drunk, she knew what she was doing. "Can I have the key babe?" Stunned, Max handed it over and she walked off to the lift with the two guys she had only just met. She looked back at Max as she entered the lift and then the doors closed and she was gone.

Max sipped his drink for a few minutes, stood up, went to his car, got in and drove off. He left his stuff at the Hotel including the engagement ring he had bought. He never saw Miranda again, never enquired about her, couldn't give a shit what happened to her. It was from that moment, that he now had no interest in any girl.

Max wiped away his tears; he had really loved Miranda, he had wanted to be with her and wanted her to be his only one. His heart had been completely broken, and he now had no sex drive; not even an urge. The image of Miranda with those two men and what they would have done to her, was all consuming. If *she* could change like that; from a sweet innocent girl he had met at sixteen, God knows what these other experienced girls were like.

***

Pete laughed as they walked into his house. "Shit man, that girls face when we said 'Yeah, we know the price of a glass. We want the fucking bottle!'

"And their fucking faces when we only had one glass and gave the fucking bottle away to some random lads." Geezer laughed. "Nine hundred fucking quid the bottle." He put his hand up and high fived Pete.

"Go on into the living room Geez. What do you fancy to drink?" Pete asked.

"Campari and Tonic water, would be lovely." Geezer boomed.

"Sophie, can you get a Campari and Tonic water for Geezer and I'll have a tonic water, ice and lemon. You want ice Geezer?"

"Yeah." Geezer said. "I'll have some ice, sexy." He called out to Sophie, who had gone into the kitchen. "Nice bird mate, nice tits, arse, legs, nice lips, nice all over. Where did you find her?"

"Usual mate, Sloane Square, same as the last one."

"Not that one you got in the fuck films now, you dirty bastard. The guys showed me the other day. Couldn't believe it, she was getting it all ways from a bunch of guys."

"Yeah, I know, I got bored of her, she got too big for her fancy boots, so I passed her down the food chain."

"And this one?"

"Bored." Pete winked.

"Already? You ready to pass her down then?" Geezer smiled, feeling his cock harden.

"You do me the right deal, and I'll give her to you tonight." Pete smiled and raised his glass. "You stiff me, and you get nothing from me and the deal's over."

"OK, OK." Geezer smiled. "What do you want?"

Pete looked at Geezer and smiled. Geezer was from a poor estate in Manchester, he was a half-cast, but he didn't know where the half came from. He knew his mother was Indian but he didn't know what his dad was he could of been black, white, or Chinese, but one thing he was certain of; was that his dad was not Indian. His mother had been out-cast from the family for being pregnant out of wedlock, and not with an Asian man. She had had to bring up Geezer, nicked-named from the age of twelve for being a 'Geezer' as he was the man of the house without a father. His mother had said it once in front of the school gates one day and it had stuck. She had worked multiple jobs to earn some money on the side, dropping her knickers to office workers during her cleaning jobs, and shagging the odd supermarket manager, until she got too old. By the time Geezer was fourteen, he was a street-dealer, by the time he was sixteen, he was running a group of street-dealers, at nineteen he killed his first supplier. At twenty-one, he owned his block, then his estate, then his territory. He had killed four people by the age of twenty-four and had not been caught. No one gave a shit, the police did routine enquiries, but most people who played this game didn't give a shit if the money kept flowing up the food chain. If the big guys got paid, they didn't give a fuck what happened in the school yard, as they called, the estates. Geezer made sure the big boys got paid and on time.

"You're coming here from Manchester, bypassing London and supplying me in Maidstone direct?" Pete enquired.

"Correct. You haven't got a dealer here; London has missed you out as small fry." Geezer stated.

"Oh. How comes you see us then?" Pete asked. "Why, you interested, if London thinks we're too small?"

"Your band, Yellow Snow, I've seen them on the TV and in the papers, the next big thing apparently. You're getting all the kids down here because of them, and you've a booming weekend night scene, and also a Sunday-lunch band scene. I want the drugs deals in your club. You put one of my guys in Hospital last month, now he can't speak properly, probably never will again." Geezer moaned.

"No one told *me* anything!" Pete defended himself. "You know I don't like drugs, I don't touch them and have no respect for those who do. But, if you have a dealer in my club without telling me, and not paying his dues on the deals, of course I'm going to hit him."

Geezer laughed. "I've had a word about the disrespect and now he also has a knee to worry about. He should've told you and rented his turf. I agree it's his own fault he got hit. But now we are here to agree a pitch." Geezer stated as he took a cigarette out of its packet and lit it. "Anyway, Pete, you should let your hair down and try some chemicals, cocaine makes your dick hard and the girls go wild on the stuff."

"I Don't need it and don't like it, Geezer. That's not to say I have anything against people that do, what you do is your call. I just won't touch it." Pete explained.

"What about your little lady, does she touch it?" Geezer smiled.

"Ask her when she gets back, she'll be gone a while. She has to get the tonic from the garage."

"I will." Geezer smiled. "Makes them horny Pete, makes them fuck hard and filthy."

"OK Geezer. The deal, this is what I want; 40% of sales in the club. Only known dealers to me *in* the club, no harassment to my punters, and all drugs dropped in a stash point, so *if* we get raided, I can prevent the police getting anywhere near it."

"35%."

"45% if you are going to make this hard for me."

"OK 40%."

"45%, you did make it hard for me. And, my team strip and search the money takers and take our cut on the night. You try doing any switching in the night or have any other couriers, we'll take the lot and put all your guys in hospital, even if they are girls."

"Alright Pete, deal." Geezer smiled. "But for fuck's sake, calm down on the violence. Let's make some money and have some peace."

Pete shook Geezers hand and smiled. "Try and fuck me over Manc' and I *will* hurt you."

"Alright… easy, agreed. Now let's talk about sexy Sophie." Geezer smiled as he let Pete's hand go. "I'm a lover not a fighter."

"All yours, you can have her tonight, all night, I've plenty of spare rooms upstairs, do what you want with her." Pete smiled.

"Really?" Geezer asked. "To tell you the truth. I fancy fucking her in front of you. I want you to see what a good northern half-chap cock can do to a posh southern white bird."

"Geezer, she's all yours. If you want to double-up on her, we can, but I really have no fucking wish or want for that girl to be anywhere near me right now."

"So why is she here tonight then?" Geezer asked. "A gift for you Geezer, she doesn't know it yet though, she thinks I'm well into her. Let's see what we can get her to do for you, shall we?"

Geezer smiled, rubbed his hands together and pulled out a bag of white powder. "You're a bad arse." Geezer slapped his arm. "Let's try her on the happy powder."

Pete rolled his eyes, but Geezer smiled. They sat there listening to the music on the hi-fi. Pete had found some middle of the road CD and they sat back and waited for Sophie to return with the drinks.

Carrying a bottle of Campari, tonic water and a bottle of wine, she smiled at both men as she entered the room. Geezer sat in the middle of the sofa and Pete in the lounge chair. She wore a flowy dress with a low plunging neckline down to her waist, no bra and no knickers, as Pete had demanded, and as she made her way to the sideboard to pour the drinks, Pete winked and Geezer. Returning and serving the drinks in front of both men, her top bellowed has she leant forward completely revealing her breasts.

"Sophie my lovely, go and sit down next to Geezer." Geezer slapped the leather sofa beside him. "I have a little surprise for you."

Sophie looked at Pete, who smiled and nodded. Sophie sat down and as she did her skirt rose up a bit and she automatically pulled it back down.

Geezer held up his plastic bag of cocaine and put it on the coffee table in front of Sophie. "Ever tried this stuff?"

Sophie smiled, "A couple of times, not that much though."

"Would you like to try some? It makes you relax and have a good time." Geezer encouraged as he poured some of the contents of the bag onto the table.

"I am having a good time." Sophie smiled.

"Well this will just be the icing on the cake."

"Shall I Pete?" Sophie turned to Pete. Pete sat there and thought 'If you knew my stand point on drugs you would not even ask that question, you stupid whore.' "Sophie darling, you only regret the things you don't do."

Sophie smiled. "OK Geezer, I'll try a little bit." Geezer winked at Pete, who raised his eyebrow, shaking his head in disbelief.

"Right babe, now this is how it's done." He poured some cocaine onto the glass table and leant down next to it, pulled out his wallet and his gold American express card. He divided and cut into the powder and separated it, cut it again, then organised it into four lines. He pulled out a fifty pound note and rolled it into a tube, placed it at the end of one line and snorted along it, then passed it to Sophie. "Now your turn." She kneeled at the table, snorted a line and sat back, she pulled a face like she had just eaten a lemon and then smiled. "That's it, now snort the next up the other side." Geezer snorted the last line and they both relaxed back on the sofa together.

For a while, they enjoyed a light-hearted evening with general chat, laughter and music, then Geezer put his hand on Sophie leg. "You are a very sexy young lady, Sophie; you have a very fit body." He rubbed his hand up her thigh and Sophie didn't seem to resist. "I would love to see those breasts of yours in the flesh."

Sophie looked at Peter and giggled. "No you can't, don't be silly!"

"You must have gone topless on the beach? It's only me and Pete here. I'm sure he won't mind, would you Pete, it's just like being on the beach, come on, let pretend we're on the beach!"

Sophie giggled and looked at Pete. "Go on Sophie, Geezers a good friend of mine, we're partners. He'll make us a lot of money. He only wants to see your tits."

Sophie giggled and stood up. She looked at Pete for reassurance, then at Geezer and then back at Pete who smiled and nodded. Swaying to the beat, she lowered her top to her waist and revealed her breasts.

"Now they *are* magnificent Sophie." Geezer praised. "Now come back and sit next to me."

Sophie giggled and plonked herself next to Geezer who leant over and put a hand on her firm breast, squeezing it hard. The locked his lips onto hers and kissed her deeply. Sophie responded by kissing him back. Geezer then put his hand up her skirt and cupped her vagina and rubbed it passionately, then immediately pushed his finger into her hard.

Sophie suddenly realised what was happening and pushed back and struggled out of his grasp. "No Geezer, I'm with Pete."

"Pete don't mind Sophie. Look at Pete he doesn't mind."

Sophie turned to look for Pete reaction, he smiled and then said. "Sophie, Geezer is all the way down from Manchester and I didn't sort anything out for him."

"What?" Sophie asked. "You don't mind. That your friend wants to fuck me?"

"Sophie sweetheart, we are all friends here. No, I'm not going to let him fuck you, we are both going to fuck you, you are my one and only, remember? Do you like that idea?"

Sophie looked at the two of them in turn and smiled. "If you don't mind. I don't mind."

With that Geezer quickly pushed her back on the Sofa and parted her legs, he pulled his cock out and pushed it into her. Pete watched them for a few minutes while Geezer pounded her and she panted and squealed, then he moved over to the sofa, dropped his own trousers and grabbed Sophie by the head and put his cock in her mouth. She sucked and moaned for a while, then Geezer looked at Pete and winked.

"Let me turn her over Pete."

Geezer pulled out of her and turned her around so that she could sit on Pete's cock. She rode him for a while, then Pete pulled her forward onto his chest, spreading her arse with his hands. Geezer moved forward and placed his cock between her arse cheeks and pushed himself in. Sophie squealed out loud and bucked in Pete's arms, then relaxed as there was no mistake Geezer was in and fucking her arse hard, Pete held her solidly on his cock.

***

Pete woke alone in the morning; he had given Sophie to Geezer. Sophie had had a few more lines and Geezer just didn't seem to ever be satisfied. Pete had gone to bed around midnight and had left them to it.

He switched on his TV, pressed the source button and flicked through some options which showed each room of the house. The TV was linked to the house security and Pete had chosen to put a camera in each room including the bedrooms; he had recordings of every guest that had ever stayed. In the image on channel twelve, Geezer was rutting Sophie from behind; she lay flat on the bed and he had her pinned from above. Pete smiled and switch the TV off, got up, had a shower and left the house to go to the club.

Chapter 9

Max spoke into the phone. "They're a local band, young kids from Maidstone Grammar School. They're in the finals of the Battle of the Bands competition, with an opportunity to work with a proper record producer and perform at the KOKO in London if they win."

He listened and then added. "If you provide a bus, I'll make sure the local press and radio gets a story that it was you that helped these kids out." There was a pause again. "I'll be going with them on the bus, along with two other adults." Another pause. "Yes, any damage will be paid for." Pause "That's great, thank you." Max hung up and smiled.

The local bus firm had given him a bus to ship fifty plus kids from Maidstone to Tonbridge for the final of the Battle of the Bands. They had stormed through every round, but he needed to make sure that they nailed the final. It was all down to votes and this was a big one. Since he had started on this journey, he had really found his feet and had enjoyed the challenge. The band had played all the best venues in the area and was now resident in the Basement. They would now be the 'headliners' with two guest bands in every month. Pete loved it. The place was banged-out at least once and month when Yellow Snow played, and the remaining three music nights were growing in popularity. Pete had given him the Wednesday night, which was not the best, obviously he had been after a Friday night, but one of the other more important guys involved in the club, wanted to keep it as a disco night.

The Battle of the Bands competition was a week away and he wanted to win it.

***

It was a cold night. The bus had arrived at Moat Park and the kids were all standing around. There was more than expected and he had to keep the figures to the capacity of the bus. He had fifty-seven seats, which meant fifty-four kids. Carol and her friend Dawn were joining him to help look after the kids. There must have been more than sixty kids wanting to go. So he lined them up and then counted them onto the bus, while Carol and Dawn removed bags of alcohol and placed them on the grass behind them. Once all fifty-four kids were counted on, there must have been twenty kids left over. "Sorry, but that's it. Have any of you got any way of getting there, mum's, dad's?" Max asked.

Some of the kids moaned, some were on their mobiles. Max picked up the bags of alcohol and put them in the back of Carol's car, returned to the bus and got on. The door closed behind him and they were off.

The kids were noisy and in good spirits, all in all it was a fun trip, the journey was around forty minutes and the bus pulled up at the bottom of the hill near 'The Forum'.

The kids piled off and most made their way to the venue, while others headed towards the town, probably to source more alcohol to replace what had been previously confiscated. Max made his way into the club followed by Carol and Dawn.

At the door, they had explained who they were, and all three received a black stamp on their wrists. The place was already hot and full of kids; the first band was setting-up on stage. Max knew that Yellow Snow had arrived a few hours earlier, so they made their way backstage to find them, the lead singer was chatting-up young girls and the rest of the band members were sitting around tuning their instruments.

As they entered the dressing rooms, the band acknowledged Max, but with no real warmth, 'They were too cool for that' Max thought, but Carol didn't even get a look in either. Max found Adam and asked him what time they were on. 'second to last' he was told. Which was good.

"So, have a good show and I'll see you after." Max told him. Adam just grinned.

Max turned to Carol. "I don't think they want us adults here. Shall we go and find a wine bar and come back just before they come on?"

"Sounds good to me." And they made their way out.

***

The venue was now swelteringly hot; Max was sweating. The place was packed, Max stood with Carol and Dawn at the back. The last band had finished ten minutes ago and the place was getting ready for Yellow Snow. The lights dimmed and he watched the band walk onto the stage and take their positions, the compere announced. "Please Welcome to the stage, from Maidstone, the one and only... Yellow Snow."

The band broke into their opening guitar rift, followed by the drums, then they all joined in along with the countdown of the lead singer. The place erupted and they were off.

Their set lasted twenty minutes and as they played, Max watch both Carol and Dawn dance about on the spot, even his feet were tapping. 'Shit these kids were good' he thought. He really started to enjoy himself.

Once their set had finished to a crescendo of applause Max, Carol and Dawn made their way out into the fresh air. "Now that was good." Max said. "I think they have a chance of winning, you know."

"What *do* they win?" Dawn asked.

"They get a proper producer to make them a five track EP and they get to play at 'KOKO' in London with other up and coming acts."

"Wow, that's cool." Dawn said. "A London gig. That will be good for them, won't it Carol."

Carol smiled. "Yes, that's what they wanted and it's all down to Max here. He's done a wonderful job." Max looked at her and smiled. Pete had asked him what their actual chance of winning was, while he reminded him that Carol owed him a good shag if they got to London.

"Shall we go for another drink and come back in forty minutes for the results?" Max asked.

***

Back in the 'Venue' half an hour later, the main organiser was on the stage thanking the sponsors and the bands for being there and emphasising the fact that the incredible journey so far had whittled down over 300 initial bands, to the last remaining four. Then he began to call out the votes. "The Neptune 153 votes, The Kramps 124 votes, Neckline 83 votes and with a clear winner of over 200 votes with a total of 254 votes is... Yellow Snow!"

The kids cheered and Yellow Snow came out onto the stage to receive a glass trophy and to have their photographs taken. A journalist was also on stage to interview them, recording their every word. Once the excitement had slowed down, the band moved off and the main lights came on.

"Well done Max!" Dawn smiled.

"Yes, bloody well done. I couldn't have done that. And well done for sorting out the bus; that was a brilliant idea."

As they walked out he heard a disgruntled kid say to his mate. "They only won cos they got a manager and he sorted them out a bus." Max smiled and thought 'That's right you little shit.'

Max's phone went off in his pocket. "Yes Pete, they won." Pete then hung up and within a second Carol's phone rang. She answered it. "Yes, I know, yes. It is good news, yes..., I will come over tomorrow evening." With that she hung up.

***

Pete was all smiles when Max walked into his office. "Well done my son. What happens next?"

"Well, they get their EP done by a professional studio and by a renowned producer. They get given 250 copies and the master."

"So we can sell them?" Pete asked.

"Yes." Max said. "And make more copies."

"OK. Good. We'll make some cash there then. When are they in London?"

"End of the month."

"Good, Good. I've Carol coming here at two o'clock. She has her part of the deal to do and I'm a fucking horny sod today." He smiled. "You never thought of doing her?"

"What, No. Anyway, she's too old for me Pete."

"Too old? What is it with you? You gay son?" Pete asked.

"No, Pete." Max Moaned. "I'm not gay."

"I don't care if you are. It doesn't bother me."

"I just can't be bothered. I put a lot of time into a girl once and she just played me like a bloody idiot." Max dropped his eyes to the floor.

"Fuck'em mate." Pete snarled. "That's what I do. Some fucking little rich bitch thought she was too good for me when I was about your age." He paused as he thought. "Now look at me. I could buy the little fucking slag out, all her family and put them on the street. I thought about doing it a while ago. Buying her dad's firm and then just shutting the fucking thing down, but it would have meant giving the fuckers the money."

"I've just have not found a girl I can trust." Max stated.

"Fuck me son, you just need to fuck them, not marry them."

"Yeah, but I'm just not that way inclined." Max said.

"Well, if you hang around here about two this afternoon, you'll hear a certain little lady paying for your success."

"Yeah, I think I'll pass on that."

"Thanks again mate, You're a star." Pete smiled.

"You're welcome, Pete."

***

Max looked at the clock on his office wall and decided he was going to call it a day. It was coming up to two o'clock and he really didn't want to be in his office while Pete was entertaining Carol. He shut his computer down, got up and walked out. At the entrance doorway to the club, he passed her coming the other way. He just nodded to her, she nodded back and he left the building.

***

Pete made himself comfortable on his sofa ready for his anticipated fun to begin, he had a bottle of champagne chilling in an ice bucket and two glasses ready. There was a faint knock on the door and Denise from the bar showed in Carol. Pete smiled and invited her to sit next to him.

"Now for Champers to celebrate your young lad's success." He touched Carol's knee. "Here's to the little kids and my man Max." He leant over popped the cork and poured two glasses, passing one to Carol, raising his glass to connect with hers he toasted "To my man and your little band."

Carol smiled nervously as she took a sip of her drink.

"Smile and enjoy yourself, Carol, we both know why you're here, a deal is a deal."

Carol still responded with a nervous smile.

"Come on, you know this will be fun." Pete moved his hand up her thigh. "Now, why don't you take your top off."

Carol looked at him. "Pardon?"

"Take your top off Carol. I want to see your nice tits."

Carol leant forward and removed her jacket, then her blouse and then her bra.

"Now that's nice. You have lovely tits Carol." Pete grabbed a breast and then tweaked her nipple. He then moved his hand up her thighs to her knickers, pulled them to one side and slid a finger into her. "See, I told you, you'd like it; you're wet already." Pete started to finger her and felt her relax. He slid in another finger and then reached under for her anus.

"No Pete." Carol moaned. "I don't do anal."

"What do you mean you don't do anal?" Pete snapped.

"I don't do it."

"What do you mean, you don't do it?" Pete laughed.

"I've been married to Kevin for fifteen years and he's not into sex, so I've not done it for years." She moaned.

"Kevin has never back doored you?" Pete laughed again. "Never tried?"

"No, he has never tried."

"Well, Carol, you're in for a treat this afternoon, and so it seems am I, as we are going to re-introduce your arse to a good fucking."

"No Pete, that's not the agreement. You said I would have to let you fuck me if they got to London."

"Yes, and fucking to me is your arse too."

"No, Pete, you said I would have to do anything you wanted if they got *signed*." Carol moaned.

"Yes, lover anything." Pete smiled a nasty smile. "Anything means anything I want. Fucking your arse in my book is fucking, like I just said. Fucking anything, is if I want to take pics of you. If I want to watch you fuck someone. If I want to gangbang you with my mates. If I want you to fuck some random stranger. I tell you. Your arse will be used when we play those games. I will want you to DP."

"Pete, no I won't do it." Carol moaned.

"Yes, you will, or otherwise your kid's band dies a death and Kevin will find out about our little rendezvous."

"Pete, you wouldn't" Carol snapped.

"Er, Yes, I would." Pete smiled again. "Now have some champers and get those clothes off."

Carol picked up her glass. "Pete, please don't do this."

"Never break a deal, Carol." Pete put his hand back up her skirt. "And in reality, you know you're just teasing, cos really I know you want this." Pete smiled as he pulled his hand to his lips. "Look you're soaking. Now stand up and get your kit off."

Carol stood and stepped out her clothes and sat back down again. "That's it, now sit back and open up those gorgeous legs."

Carol relaxed back on the sofa and did as he asked. Pete slid three fingers into her and slid his thumb into her anus. "Now, relax Carol. You're going to love this."

Carol moaned and exhaled, as she gave in.

***

Pete panted as he removed his cock from Carol's arse. Carol fell forward and he sat back on the sofa. "I told you, you would like that. I felt you cum before I did."

Carol didn't say anything. She turned and stood up, picking up her clothes.

"What are you doing?" Pete asked. "I've not finished yet."

Carol looked at him. "But?"

"But what? We finish when I'm finished. Now sit yourself back down and have another glass. I'm feeling fucking randy."

Chapter 10

The guitar riffs filled the studio, the sound engineer turned a few knobs on the extensive sound desk that banked one side of the room. There were at least forty-eight channels on the desk each controlled separately. The more knobs the engineer turned the unhappier he looked, the producer sat deflated and bored. "For fuck's sake, can't that kid keep up the same timing for more than an hour. He keeps losing it."

"Stop, stop, stop." The producer shouted into the microphone. Carl the bass player, looked up in frustration. "Get out of that fucking room, go to the back room and fucking practice how to play your instrument, you Cunt!"

Max smiled. It had been like this all day. Keith was a perfectionist and had produced some of the best bands that had come out of England. They were on a little island in the Thames called Platts Eyot. The studio had been designed and built by the sound engineer with the money he had earned from a top ten hit, he had had with his band in the early 90's.

Keith turned to Max. "Get that fucking bassist in here and make sure he can play. This is all costing me money. I'm making them a five track EP and if it has my *NAME* to it, it has to be good." He rolled his eyes. "Fuck knows why I agreed to this, I must have been pissed, probably was, cunts."

Max smiled and walked out of the sound room and into the back room where the band were sitting about moping and moaning. "That guy in there is a fucking up-himself twat!" Moaned Adam.

"Lads, this is for free and that 'up-himself twat' as you put it, is one of the best guys in the business. So, welcome to the world of music." Max smiled. "What did you expect? He's doing his job and he's trying to get the best out of you."

"Yeah, but he says we can't play, can't keep rhythm. We have been on this for hours, how are we supposed to keep rhythm hour after hour?" Adam moaned. "The guys are really pissed off."

"Hey, this is the job, what do you think being a musician is about?" Max tried to encourage them. "Just relax and let him do his stuff. You'll love the tracks you get. You want a shot at the big time? Then you need this EP. Once you have it, you will have something for the record labels to look at."

"Yeah, I know that, but he doesn't need to be like he is. Plus, he's a piss head; he stinks of booze when he gets in, in the morning." Adam moaned.

"Look, just go along with it." Max told Adam, "Carl, he wants you in now."

Carl looked up, grabbed his Bass and headed out the room without a word. Max liked Carl. Out of all the members of the band, he was the one that was happy to just do what he was told. Max wished the rest of the band were like that. The worst members were the singer and the drummer; rich kids from rich families that never had to do a hard day's work in their lives.

***

Pete and Mike both smiled as they looked at the computer screen. The image showed Carol bent over Pete's desk. "This is the moment I fucked her arse. Look at her face, all worried. Then I'm in, look how her face changes now. She is loving it. I tell you, she came hard in about a minute."

Mike turned to Pete. "She is one fit lady for her age and she's had a kid."

"Yeah, she's a babe. I'm wondering if she'll be back for more. I'll leave it a few weeks so she can think about it and then give her a call. I tell ya she loved it. If our Max works his miracles with the band, I might even let you have a go."

Mike smiled. "I wouldn't say no. Thanks."

Pete changed the screen on the computer to an accounts spreadsheet. "Now, I'm just going through the accounts..." Pete now looked serious.

"The websites are good, the Credit Card swipes are good, the Club takings on music nights are good, these are due to Max. The Club takings on Friday & Saturday night are shit, the car clamping at the pub is shit, the bar takings *in* the club are shit, burger vans, money going missing, or we are suddenly doing shit. Do you wanna explain?"

"Pete, Max has got everything sewn up. He's such a hard worker and I've got a good feeling about him, he cannot but fail." Mike moaned.

"Mike, you are supposed to be my right hand man, don't tell me about Max and what he is doing." Pete snarled. "What are you doing about your shit?"

Chapter 11

Max sat behind his desk and stared at each teenager who formed Yellow Snow. Each one sat with a big grin on their face, as Max fiddled with their CD in his hand. It was the five track demo, that already had people interested. The studio time had eventually gone well, even with the arrogant attitude of the little kids and the half pissed producer. In the end it was that very same piss-head producer that had actually liked the sound and feel of the band and had kindly passed some of the tracks around to some of his mates in the industry. Not only had people liked it, but it had even had some air-play. X-FM had played a track, Radio 2 late night had played it a couple of times and this had generated some brilliant local press for the band.

They were becoming local stars, but with that, their arrogance began to grow.

"This is going down well boys." Max smiled as he held the CD high in the air. "There is a new TV channel called The Musicians Channel that has just started broadcasting on one of the Sky Channels. Nothing big, but I have just come off the phone to them and they want to record two of your tracks for their channel."

The band looked at him, then the lead singer hit the drummer on the arm and sniggered. "Fucking hell! That's great." Carl beamed. "When's this going to happen?"

"Well... if you can get the day off. Thursday." Max smiled.

"Shit, really?" The band sort of said in unison.

"Yep, really. We also have some gigs being lined up. It's not going to be long lads and we will have a record label knocking...."

***

By the end of the week Pete was smiling, Max had told him about the TV studio recording of the band and the list of gigs that Yellow Snow was now booked in for. "I have also got some interest from some festivals for the summer months."

"That is great Max." Pete smiled. "Anything I can do to help?"

"If you know anyone who has a minibus. I could do with some transport for the lads."

Pete looked at Max. "Max with the money you're making. Why don't you just buy one?"

"I don't want a new one. I want a good, reliable second hand one." Max explained.

"OK. I'll see what I can do." Pete told him.

As Max left Pete's office, Pete picked up the phone, and pressed one of the speed dial digits. He waited a couple of seconds before saying. "Hi, Carol, the boys seem to be doing rather well. I hear they're about to go on the TV. I think it's time we had another get together." With that, he hung up and smiled.

***

Max accelerated up the road in his minibus. It was a couple of years old, ford transit in dark blue and had cost him £10K. He quite liked it and to his surprise it was quite nice to drive. The lads were settled in the back generally messing about as typical teenagers do, only thinking of themselves with not a lot else to worry about.

He indicated left, and then called out. "Right lads, stop pissing about, we're coming up to the studio entrance."

Meridian TV Studios were based in Maidstone, which was handy, just off a roundabout on the edge of a housing estate. He pulled up to the barrier and a uniformed security guard came to his window.

"Yellow Snow, for the Musicians Channel." Max explained.

The security guard looked down his clipboard, pulled a pen out and marked them off. "OK, follow this road round to the right and park up in the visitor's car park. When you get to reception ask for Angela."

"Great, thanks." Max smiled and as the barrier was lifted, he drove as instructed to the visitor's car park.

Reaching the parking bay, he turned off the engine and turned to the lads in the back. "Right lads, no dicking around, listen to what they have to tell you, and do what you're told." He looked at the lads faces, who all seemed excited. "Everyone in this building knows what they're doing, even if they are fat, ugly or a pisshead, so be respectful."

The lads laughed and got out the bus. They made their way to the reception where Max asked for Angela. The receptionist, studied the lads to see if she recognised them, decided she didn't and then disinterested asked them to sign the visitors book and issued each of them with a plastic badge holder in which they slipped in their paper visitors slip. They were asked to wait in reception while they waited for Angela to turn up to collect them.

The lads fidgeted with excitement glancing around the reception and studying the various pictures that hung on the walls of different famous TV personalities. Within a couple of minutes, a young, dark haired girl in a white blouse and blue jeans arrived and asked if they were Max with Yellow Snow.

Max stood, smiled and walked over to her and shook her hand.

"Hi, Angela, I'm Max, and they are Yellow Snow."

"Yeah, Hi guys." Angela smiled. "I Liked your demo and your look. You guys should be pretty popular pretty soon."

The band smiled at her. "So, let's go up to the canteen where you guys can get some breakfast and we can get the legal stuff signed off."

She led the way to the stairs and walked up to the first floor and into the canteen.

"Have what you want, while I get the contracts sorted out."

Carl looked nervous. "What is it Carl?" Max asked.

"How much does this cost, I've got no money." Carl moaned.

"Carl, you're the stars here." Max smiled. "It doesn't cost anything, it's free."

The drummer and singer laughed and punched each other in the arm and headed for the serving plates, which they filled with the full English Breakfast. Max just had a black coffee and waited for Angela to return; this was the first time that he had spoken to someone on the phone who had actually looked better in the flesh than he had imagined. He had surprised himself, checking her out as she walked through the door to leave. He felt slightly excited in the anticipation of her return.

The lads were sitting at another table, leaving Max to himself, which always made him smile; why they never came and sat with him always surprised him, but he let it be. They were a good ten years younger than him so he understood that he must have seemed like a father figure to them. As he took another sip of his coffee, Angela returned with a folder under her arm and a handful of pens. She walked over to Max and took the seat opposite him. "OK then, Max." She smiled. "This is the paperwork. There is a contract for each of the band members to sign."

"Can you just give me an executive summary of the contract content, before I read through and then get the lads to sign?" Max asked.

Angela looked at Max and smiled. "You're the first person to have ever ask what's in the contract." She paused as she looked at Max, then continued. "This is a new channel, with a new idea. The Musicians channel's concept is to get unsigned bands noticed on a media format of the Sky Platform. We broadcast the videos of the bands that we record here, in the hope that they will go on to bigger and better things. The contract just states that we have the copyright and broadcast rights to the video, to be used in any way we see fit in the future. In a sense, if the band goes on to bigger and better things, we have an initial video we can do with as we wish."

"Do we get a copy of the video?" Max asked.

"Yes, I'll give you a VHS copy." Angela stated.

"Sounds OK to me. Just let me read through quickly and I'll get the lads to sign it off."

Max took one of the contracts off of Angela and started reading, as she made her way over to the band and started making light hearted conversation. Max looked over the contract; there was nothing there to be concerned about. They were not being paid, they would hold all the rights to the songs, but allowed the image of the video to be used as the station saw fit. He couldn't see anything that concerned him, so went over to the table and asked the lads to sign. They all did without question, apart from Adam, whom quite rightly asked about the rights to the songs. He was the songwriter so of course had the right to ask. After a few words from Max and Angela, Adam duly signed.

***

Max sat in the control room with the producers of the new music channel. The room was filled to capacity with eight or so people coming and going, there were various monitors on the wall, on the desks and a large viewing window into the performance room. They had so far, recorded three songs, and had repeated them over and over again, from different angles, on different instruments, and also focusing on each individual artist. It had all been fun and games for the first few hours, but now the lads were flagging; their smiles were gone and every time they came to the end of a track, the singer's face showed that he wanted to call it a wrap. Max was pleased when finally, one of the producers turned to him and said. "I think we have it now. Not bad these lads, I think they may have a good chance."

"Could you let them go for a couple more takes?" Max said. "I want them to learn this is not an easy game to be in." Angela looked at Max and then back to the recording booth.

"OK." The producer smiled. "But we won't record and those of you that want to go home can."

Angela smiled. "I'll stay Jeremy." Jeremy called into the mic in front of him. "OK, from the top lads, make this a good one and we'll call it a day."

Max smiled as the lead singer shrugged, threw his arms down, and as the first rifts of the track were played, he started to sing in earnest. If anything the guy was a professional and enjoyed what he did.

"They're not bad, the best we've had in here for a while." Angela said.

"Really, you like this sort of music?" Max asked.

"Yes…. I'm a bit of a rock chick." She smiled.

"You should come down to the club in town, on a Wednesday. I have a regular night there, putting on the local unsigned bands from the area."

"Um, I'd like that." She smiled. "I'll defiantly come down, I'll bring a friend."

"Yeah, sure." Max replied, wondering who her friend was, hoping in the back of his mind, that it was not her boyfriend. Angela was called over to the control desk by Jeremy and as she walked away, Max sat back in his chair, watching her move across the room; he put his arms behind his head and smiled.

***

Pete sat in his office, on his sofa waiting for the knock on the door. "Enter." He called and Carol walked in wearing a pink blouse and a short pink skirt. "Hi there, come sit down." Pete smiled. "Your boys have done well." He paused as Carol sat next to him. He immediately slid his hand up the side of her thigh to check if she had done what he had requested. "Good girl, no knickers." He turned and kissed her on the cheek and then checked her blouse, "And no bra, well done."

Carol sat back and let him grope her breast for a while. "So, your boy is on the telly now, our man Max is doing well."

Carol stayed silent.

"Here I have a copy of it, I recorded it the other day." Pete picked up a remote from the table and turned on the TV and pressed play. "They're looking good Carol."

Carol didn't speak, she just sat back, as Pete put his hand up her thigh and she obligatory opened her legs. "Good girl, you're starting to learn how our game plays. Now suck me off, while I watch your boy being famous."

Carol stayed silent as she leant over, opened Pete's trousers pulled his cock out and started sucking. Pete sat back and held her head, it didn't take long before he came in her mouth. "Thank you Carol." He stood up and put his cock back in his trousers. "Right then, now we're off on a little trip."

"What?" Carol exclaimed.

"We're off on a little trip. I said I wanted you to spend the evening with me so off we go."

Carol stood up and followed him out of his office without saying a word.

***

For the majority of the journey Carol's skirt was up around her waist and Pete had had his hand up Carol's wet vagina. She had laid back in the seat and let him with no complaint. Even when they had stopped at traffic lights parallel to a lorry driver, she had kept her legs wide open, giving the driver a full X-rated view.

"Here we are!" Pete said as they pulled into a Premier Inn hotel.

"What are we doing here Pete?" Carol asked. "If you wanted to fuck me, we could have used your office like last time."

Pete said nothing and just got out and she followed him. He entered the reception and passed the receptionist, pulling out an electronic key-card out of his pocket. They then made their way to the first floor where Pete then stopped outside room 26 and let himself in.

"Hi, Depesh?" Pete called out and as Carol walked into the room, she saw a fat, suited, middle aged Asian man sitting in a chair, sipping a glass of wine.

"Hello Pete!" Depesh smiled. "So, this is the lovely lady you spoke about."

"Yes, this is the delicious Carol." Pete had his arm around Carol's waist. "Carol, meet Depesh."

"Hello Carol. Lovely to meet you." Depesh said excitedly.

"Hello." Carol said under her breath.

"Don't be like that Carol." Pete smiled. "Depesh here, runs a big media company, and part of that media company, owns half the radio stations in the UK."

Depesh smiled. "Yes, we do. We own the airwaves." He laughed.

"Now Carol, there *is* a reason why I've bought you here to meet Depesh. If you choose to be nice to him, your son's little band will get on the radio and be played all over the country, now that would be nice wouldn't it."

Carol looked at Pete, and then Depesh. He was overweight, but looked stylish in his suit; well-groomed and a bit glazed-eyed from the wine.

"Yes, Carol, I like your band, Yellow Snow. I think they're good." He looked Carol up and down. "I can be good for them, if you are good for me." He smiled.

"Come on then, Carol." Pete smiled and smacked her on the bum. "He only wants a bit of fun, in exchange for catapulting your son's band into the spotlight."

She looked at both men with concern. "OK, I understand but do you promise this will happen?"

"Yes." They said in unison.

Carol looked at the bed and then at Depesh. "Well then Depesh, why don't you take your clothes off and get on the bed?"

"That's my girl." Pete smiled, as he sat in the chair in the corner of the room.

Depesh smiled. Stood up and removed his clothes, when he dropped his trousers Carol could not believe how long and thick his cock was for a small man. He moved over to the bed and laid on his back, his cock standing like a flag pole. Carol removed her blouse to reveal her breasts and then removed her skirt. "Keep the heels on Carol." Pete ordered from his chair.

Carol leant across the bed and let her breast slide up against Depesh's legs before putting her mouth over Depesh's cock. Depesh laid back and smiled.

Pete got up from his chair moved over to the bed and rubbed his hand between Carol's arse cheeks and then slid two fingers in her wet pussy. He was tempted to stay and fuck her.

"Hey, Depesh. Enjoy yourself and remember she likes it in the arse!" Pete laughed. "Meet me in the bar when you're done."

Pete left the room.

***

Pete sat in the bar chatting-up two housewives that seemed to be out looking for some fun. He had time on his hands, and he loved a challenge. He checked the time on his watch, in order to see how long, it would take for the flirting to evolve into some more physical. Within the hour both were trying to out-do each other, taking turns in touching his arm, his hands, and then inevitable his thigh. It was easy, the drinks he was supplying at a fast rate of knots were helping no end, and within no time at all, he was bored of it all.

While the two women were batting their eye lids and flicking their hair, he was wondering how Depesh was getting on. He smiled to himself, he had not known Depesh at all, Max had told him of this great contact he had made with the media company, and how they had liked the band so had agreed to play them across the network.

Max had been excited, as he had managed to do this by himself without the use of an industry 'plugger.' Apparently, the girl from the TV studio had put in a good word and that he had sealed the deal.

Pete had taken it upon himself to contact the media company directly and had spoken with some fella called Depesh, he had invited him down to his club, and told him about the offer he had on the table with Carol. Depesh had initially declined, until he was shown the video of Carol the night he fucked her in his office. Depesh had smiled, "Now she *is* a pretty MILF."

***

Meanwhile, upstairs, Carol sucked on Depesh's large cock; it was the largest she had experienced, it stretched her mouth as she took it in. Depesh lay back moaning, she couldn't believe what she was doing, but after the night in Pete's office, she thought why not, it was all for her son's career, it was only sex after all and something she was not getting from her husband; he just didn't seem interested anymore and was either always out or always too tired. That night in Pete's office had re-lit a fire that had not burned inside her for a while and she remembered the intense feeling of climaxing. Anal penetration was something she never imagined herself ever experiencing and after the initial apprehension, she had actually enjoyed it. Even tonight, when he had been playing with her in the car and she had seen the voyeur looking down upon them had turned her on.

Now she was with a complete stranger, she closed her eyes and just enjoyed the warmth filling her body. "Lick my balls..." she heard him moan, she let herself go in the moment, and followed his every command, she licked them, held them in her mouth and slowly sucked them. "Finger my arse baby..." he moaned again. This was new to her, but again, she did as she was told. "Another finger, yes baby...." He writhed of her fingers. "Now suck my cock...." She opened her mouth and took him as deep as she could manage. He held her head so she couldn't move. She felt his cock swell and then her mouth was full, she could only but swallow as he held her head tight against his body. He sighed and lay back. "Thank you, babe... now come here and sit on my face...."

With nervous excitement, she moved up the bed and across his body and straddled his head lowering herself onto his tongue. Her whole body went warm as his tongue probed and his lips sucked. She felt his tongue on her anus and opened her legs wider, she felt his finger in her arse then another and then she felt him stretch her with four fingers, she sat back on his fingers as his mouth sucked on her. She could feel her whole body getting hot and the hairs on her lower back rising. She was just enjoying herself, eyes still closed not looking at who was doing this to her, just enjoying the sensation, the whole experience.

"I'm ready to go again.... Sit on my cock...."

She looked behind her and his cock was again like a flag pole. She worked her way back and felt it as it stretched her as he entered. She sat back and started to ride him.

Depesh sat up, grabbed her hips and twisted her to one side, in one swift movement he was now standing at the end of the bed, pushing hard into her from behind and she found herself on all fours on the edge of the bed with his thumb already in her arse. She had already cum once and was getting sore from the pounding. Depesh withdrew and then pushed her forward face down, with his knee, he opened her legs and pushed his cock into her anus. "No... Please, no...." Carol moaned.

"Pete says you like this..."

Depesh pushed hard at her anus, he felt the muscle relax and he slid in stretching her, feeling her around his cock. "Babe you have a tight arse..."

Carol squealed with the initial pain, then relaxed as pure euphoria took over her body. She felt him start to pump her arse. "Cum in my arse baby..." She moaned.

***

"Enjoy the Prosecco Ladies." Pete smiled at the two women who were by now, quite drunk. "I have to leave, but my friend here can stay, he has a room."

Pete smiled as Depesh and Carol joined him at his table. Carol looked flush and her hair was showing the obvious signs that some kind of afternoon delights had certainly taken place.

"Depesh, this is Dawn and Lisa." Pete introduced the two housewives.

"Hello ladies, I can see you are having fun...?" Depesh smiled.

The two women giggled.

"Would you like a glass of Prosecco before we go?" Pete asked Carol. She nodded and took the glass that Pete had poured. She drank half of it in one gulp. "Thirsty?"

Carol smiled. "Are we going now Pete, I need to get home now, I have work in the morning."

Pete smiled and said "Yes, of course."

He turned to Depesh. "Have a good night and I will speak to you soon."

Depesh smiled and looked at the two women. "I'm sure I will." All three then waved at Pete and Carol as they turned to leave.

***

Pete pulled his Maserati onto the edge of the downs that over looked Bearsted. They could see out for miles on the clear night. "What are we doing here Pete?" Carol asked.

"Well, I want my fun now."

"Pete I don't think I can, that Depesh really wore me out and I'm a bit sore." Carol moaned.

"Come on Carol, this is for your son's music career. If he makes it to the big time, you probably won't have to work again. A little bit of effort now, is a future of comfort."

"Pete can I do it next time. I just want to go home and go to bed. I haven't even had a shower yet."

"Oh for fuck's sake." Pete undid his trousers. "Just suck me off and we'll be done for the night."

***

The club was half full as Max made his way down the stairs into the basement. The bar was two deep and the atmosphere seemed to be good, clean fun. The night was now frequented by the six-form type from the local schools. He had done a deal with the local authorities and he had been granted permission to hold an under-eighteens night once a month. The bar would not serve alcohol and the club would close at ten o'clock sharp.

Pete had helped him out with the jobs-worth's at the council, he had suggested they hold the meeting at the club on a Thursday night, for one good reason; it was pole-dancing night and it would give them the opportunity to offer the local authority guys some incentives. The keenest of them all, had been the headmaster of the nearest school and strangely enough, the girl he chose to entertain him, had been a previous student of his, a year earlier.

Max stood and watched the kids acting cool. The age between sixteen and eighteen always made him smile, kids were adults in one sense, but still children in another, that strange awkward transitional period into adulthood. He remembered his own time at that age, back in basic training, being a man one minute and then get excited the next because a game machine had been installed in the games room and all the lads, although now professional soldiers, went crazy for it and would spend hours trying to tag their name on the top scorers list.

Pete appeared in the room, scanned the event and then moved back into the secure area to his office. Max followed him.

"Hi, Pete," Max smiled. "How's it going?"

"All good on your front Max." Pete answered. "I wish I could get that atmosphere on a Friday and Saturday night." He scowled.

"I think you're confusing the locals with the pole-dancing night on a Thursday." Max stated. "People will automatically think we're a knocking shop."

"Isn't that a good thing?" Pete asked, with a serious face showing he was not at all joking.

"For the lads, yes. But if you want to attract the girls, it needs to be classy, or known for good music. The lads will stop coming if the place is just full of lads, or it'll become like it has of late, just a late night drinking den."

"I need some help Max." Pete seemed to plead.

Pete was right, he needed some help running the club, he was not a club owner by trade and only ran the place as a front-man, for the guy who had actually bought it.

The place was empty on a Friday and Saturday until the pubs kicked out, then it filled with lads that just wanted to get pissed until the early hours. The odd, ugly girl would come down, sometimes with a group of lads, and the presence of any women sometimes caused the squabbles; Pete's bouncers would go in heavy handed and there would be blood on the dance-floor. It had gotten a pretty bad reputation for drugs and fighting and the name 'The Basement' didn't help.

"I'm thinking of changing the name Max." Pete spoke up. "What do you think of 'B-Lo' as in below ground?"

Max smiled. "Pete I'm off to do some work. Let me have a think of some names for you." Max smiled to himself. 'What was he thinking of? 'B-Lo' the place was known as a drugs den as it was, let alone calling it one.'

As Max sat looking at the figures from the internet company. He calculated the cost of running the band against the returns they made; the returns that he still had yet to see. The costs soon added up, just to put them on tour with the minibus, the food, the beer was substantial. He made money at the club, as he owned the night and also the door and he had adopted the London bar idea, of not paying any band until they had more than fifteen on their own guest list and only then would he give them half of an entry fee for every person above the fifteen. On an average night he was earning around £750 to hold one of these nights, cash in hand and not declared that more than covered the running around of Yellow Snow to other venues; where they only earned anything between £50-£100 a night, which rarely covered the fuel, the food and drinks on the night.

He was deep in concentration when one of the girls from the bar entered.

"Hi, Max." She smiled. "There's a lady here to see you called Angela."

Max suddenly smiled. "Really?" He got up and followed Suzy to the bar.

The venue was starting to reach half capacity and the first band 'The Lonely Band' was on the stage playing to a semicircle of supporters currently lining the stage. Max turned to the bar and saw Angela standing, watching the band with a drink in her hand. He walked over and tapped her on the shoulder. She turned and smiled. "Hi!" Max shouted over the noise of the band.

Angela smiled "Hi, to you." She was wearing blue jeans, a smart blouse and a long unique looking brown and green jaded necklace. She turned to a girl that was standing with her. "Max, this is Carol, she works at the TV station with me." Her friend turned and gave an instant smile that dropped just as instantly the moment she turned back to watch the band. She was nothing like Angela, she had cropped, bleach blond hair, multiple piercings in both ears, a tattoo on the side of her neck and also on the back of her ear; a standard fashion victim who thought they were cool and original.

"Would you like another drink?" Max shouted not really knowing what else to say. He hadn't expected her to actually come down, he had asked yes, but he thought she had agreed out of courtesy.

"No. I'm fine." She held her drink up. It looked like a cola, but it could have been cola with anything. "Nice place you have here, nice atmosphere." She shouted.

"What?" Max asked. "I can't hear you for the noise." He held his hands to his ears and shook his head.

"I said…, you have a nice place here." She shouted again, exaggerating her words as though talking to a deaf person.

Max shook his head again, then leant forward. "Why don't you come to my office and we can chat there?" Angela turned and said something to her friend, who nodded, then she turned back and nodded at Max.

He led her away from the bar to the grey door with the security pad on it. He tapped in the code and they entered the dark corridor. "That's Pete's office on the left," Max pointed to the closed door. "This is mine on the right here." He tapped his new eight-digit number on the keypad; he changed it weekly and the door opened. The room already glowed a haze of blue light emanating from all his computer screens, before he turned on the main light.

"What's all this, Max?" Angela smiled. "Are you taking over the world? You need all these computers, for a band manager?"

Max grinned. "I don't just manage a band; I work on other things too. Band management doesn't pay the bills, but it's a good hobby when you don't have any hobbies."

"So what do you do?" She asked, looking around the room with more interest.

"I have my own company, making websites for other companies."

"That's interesting, what kind of companies?"

"Oh, all sorts, at the moment we have a comic book shop in the high street, most of his income comes from on-line sales now. It's quite bizarre; he gets sent comics from customers in America, then other customers from America buy them from him, so he sends them straight back to America, mad eh!"

"Why don't they just buy the comics in their own company?" She asked.

"Comics are a big thing in the US. They have a certain amount of stock to be sold in the US and Europe. When the US stock runs out they go to Europe to buy them. Most don't even come out of their wrapper. The internet shopping has opened this whole market up to your average comic book collector."

"Very strange." Angela frowned.

"And they are not kids buying them either, they are adults, collectors, fans, fanatics. It's a lot of money being traded on comic books."

"Fascinating and all done on computers now, I'm not sure about it, putting your bank details online, you never know who is getting hold of your information." She said in a cynical manner.

Max looked away, ignoring the last statement, "If you go to legitimate sites and you have good virus protection, you should be fine."

"So how did you get into this?" She pointed around the room.

"I was in the Army for ten years; Royal Signals as a Technician. I did a lot of data communications, when I worked in London for 238 Signal Squadron. They fully trained me, so when I left I put what I'd learnt into practice. Pete set me up with this office, and I have a few workers working from home, designing sites from their own houses."

"You were in the Army?" Angela looked surprised. "You don't look the Army type."

"I wasn't." Max stated. "I didn't get on that well, but it wasn't as bad as my first unit. That was a really bad place to be. Bad bullying, and all that sort of stuff. It got out of hand once, with one guy nearly murdering his Staff Sergeant on an exercise."

"What in the Army? People trying to murder each other, I can't believe that." She looked at him questioningly.

"You wouldn't believe what the army was like in the 80's, it started to change though when the press got hold of that girl that killed herself at Dipcot because of the Bullying."

"Jesus! Yeah, I think I remember that, didn't her parents complain that it was a cover up or something?"

"Yep. Anyway, what brings you here tonight?"

"I wanted to come and see Yellow Snow live in show, and come and see this club that you frequent. It has a bad name you know, people told me not to come. "Drugs, prostitution, gangsters, roughens and all that."

"Yep, that's me." Max smiled. "I'll be the roughen!"

A nervous smile appeared on Angela's lips.

"Come on then Miss, let's go and see the bands and you can see what the atmosphere is like."

Max followed Angela back into the club where she found her friend talking to a number of lads looking the same as her with piercing and tattoo's. Max never liked tattoo's or piercings, he never got the point of them and especially tattoos on kids so young, who don't really grab the concept that they are for life, but each to their own.

The second band of the night was about to finish, the crowd around the stage had grown considerably. In their final throws of climax, the drummer threw his sticks into the crowd and the band left the stage, the roar of the crowd subsided and the in-house PA came into life with rock tracks and a number of people made their way to the bar for a top-up.

"You have a great night here Max, these live music venues are few and far between nowadays." Angela said.

"I don't know, around this area there are quite a few places; Chatham, Gillingham, we have a little beach festival in Whitstable and we're booked into a few places in Margate. I've also got the guys in London, with New Cross Inn, Dublin Castle and places like that."

"You're doing well for them, are you just looking after Yellow Snow?" She asked.

"Well, I was thinking of taking some other bands on, we get some good ones in here. I get about three or four demo's posted to me a day; bands looking to play here or be represented." Max smiled. "I'm thinking of setting up 'Red Dog Promotions' as a promotions and band management company."

"Catchy name, why Red Dog?"

"Used to watch the Big Red Dog on TV when I was a kid and as you said, it's a catchy name." She smiled.

The lights dimmed as the third band made its way to the stage. The PA went quiet, there was a few cheers and the band started its set. After thirty minutes of soft punk with an indie twinge, the band finished and everyone started to get excited for the appearance of Yellow Snow.

"Angela, pardon me for a minute would you, I'll be two seconds." Max shot over to the sound desk and spoke to the sound engineer as she watched him go and return.

"What was that about?" Angela asked.

"Just making sure all the sound levels were set right for Yellow Snow. It's a little trick I've learned, always have the sound slightly-off for the support bands, that way, when the headline band comes on, they get the full system and the right settings so they always sound that much better than the bands before."

"That's not fair on the other bands, surely?" Angela looked shocked.

"That's business, people leave here talking about Yellow Snow and how they knocked the socks off all the other bands on the night." Max smiled.

After ten minutes, the lights dropped again for dramatic effect and the crowd cheered in anticipation, the drummer walked with a swagger onto the stage, sat down and started tapping his snare, the rhythm guitar player drifted on, playing a repeat rhythm, seconds after came the base player, followed by the lead guitar adding each instrument to the rhythmic beat, the lead guitarist started the rift of the first track, and as the crowd warmed up to a frenzy, the lead singer bounced on with a high octane filled scream and the band blasted into their first song. Half an hour later it ended with kids jumping up and down like pogo-sticks shouting for more.

"Max, that was amazing. Those kids really can play and entertain. Brilliant set, brilliant." Angela smiled.

"Yep, and we're still selling the demo CDs." Max indicated to a table that had been set up to the side of the stage, "We must have sold a few hundred by now. It's going really well for them, we've even got T-shirts and bits."

"It's all looking good." Angela said. "Thanks for tonight, it was good fun."

"That's OK, no problem." Max said. "You got to go?"

"Yes, I'm afraid so." Angela smiled. "I have to be up early for work tomorrow."

"OK, do you fancy meeting up away from the club?" Max heard himself ask, without even thinking.

"Yes, I think I would." Angela said. "You have my number on my email. Call me and we'll arrange something."

With that she and her friend left the club. Max smiled to himself. He quite liked her, she seemed to be the nicest girl he had met in a long time.

***

Pete looked at Mike and then down on the spreadsheet. "These figures are shit. Why are the figures on the video & DVD sales so fucking low? Why are the shops not buying the fucking stock?"

"The demand is right down, Pete." Mike moaned. "I've been speaking to everyone, the trouble is pirating, some fucker buys a film then copies it and then resells it or the punter watches free shit on the internet. The demand has dropped, plus now people are making their own films and putting them up on-line or selling it. It's one fucked-up world out there. Husbands and boyfriends are filming their wives and girlfriends and then making their own films." Mike moaned.

"Fuck it! Mike." That camera kit cost me a fucking fortune. "How's the on-line doing?"

"The on-line is dropping off as well." Mike sighed. "We've been doing everything on the live cams. We've been doing anal, gangbangs, DP's, girl on girl, multiple girl with guys, we're now fucking anything with anything. It's just dropping off." Mike looked at Pete. "There was a bloody news story on that 'Watchdog' programme, about online fraud and how to avoid being done-over. Porn sites were mentioned and since that programme we've dropped by 80%."

"Fuck it!" Pete moaned. "The fucking club is going negative, cos we ain't getting anyone in. We can't sell a fucking porno film; no fucker is watching the website. We have reduced the amount of cards we can clone, plus *that* fucking revenue has also dropped off. If I ain't got no one in the club, I can't sell any fucking drugs. Fucking hell, Mike, we need to turn this around or my fucking head will be on the fucking chopping block." Pete shouted, as he picked up his calculator from his desk and hurled it across the room.

***

Pete slammed the phone down. "Fuck... it!" He shouted out loud; his governor was not happy. There had been an investment of just under £500K into the club and as yet, they had only recouped around £300K of it. Pete had not told them about the credit card fraud, and he was now worried that someone would grass him up. And on top of it all, he had just received the news, that the Governor was sending two of his men down to 'have a chat' with him.

Pete was not entirely worried about this 'in-house gangster style potential audit' as everything had been correctly logged and the money had been flowing up the correct hill, that is apart from the credit cards section, Pete had seen this as *his* bright idea and *his* own risk, even though the websites, equipment and the filming gear had all been initially funded by The Governor.

He picked up the phone and dialled. After a couple of rings, it was answered. "Mike, I have a couple of The Governor's man coming down to audit us. I need to make sure they are entertained. Is Sophie still in good shape?" Pete listened to the answer. "Oh for fuck's sake, OK, when she's next high take her into the West End and dump her on a street somewhere. I haven't got time for her shit." He then paused. "We ain't got no other classy birds knocking about have we?"

Pete slammed the phone down. Sophie was now fully off her head and dependent. Some dozy twat had given her crack, and she hadn't come back from it. His new girl was not ready for a pass around yet, she had only just got comfortable with the odd picture and short filming on his mobile, and she was not one for drugs. He could only think of Carol. He could try and coax Carol into doing some entertaining.

He picked up his phone again and dialled Max's number and asked him to come into his office.

A couple of minutes later Max strolled in and stood at his desk.

"Take a seat Max, please." Pete told him. "How's the band doing?"

"Not bad, audiences at the club are slowly going up, and the base fans seem to be staying and coming along once a month on their guest night. CD sales are up whenever we are out and about." Max explained.

"You got any interest from any of the record label's yet?" Pete asked.

"I've a couple of nibbles, had some A & R guys coming along to some of the London gigs. It takes time, but I think we could be getting close to a call." Max smiled, pleased with himself.

Pete smiled, "Good, can you make sure the band knows."

"They do. They scan the venue every time we go out to London looking for A & R guys. They're all excited about it." Max said with a smile.

"Max." Pete said seriously. "You know our little credit card scam."

"Yes." Max answered.

"No one else knows apart from you and me do they?" Pete stared at Max.

"God, no! No one knows and I want to keep it that way." Max stated.

"Good." Pete smiled. "I want to lie-low on it for a couple of weeks, while this poxy news about scamming online is hot in the news."

"Yeah, sounds like a good idea." Max said.

"Yeah, I think so. OK well then, good..., that's all Max. I'll catch you later."

"OK."

Before Max had reached the door to leave, Pete had picked up the phone and dialled again. "Hi, Carol, it's me. Good to hear that the record label guys are sniffing around Yellow Snow..."

***

Max sat back behind his desk in deep thought, staring blankly at the figures on his screens. It was about time he got out of this office and this association he had with Pete. He had heard the gossiping in the bar, the club was failing, Pete was failing and his bosses weren't happy. There had been a lot of money invested in the club; it was supposed to have been a washing machine for dirty cash, but now there was not enough dirty-cash turning over to wash, nowhere near the amount they had planned for. Even with the backhanders, the girls and the deals, Pete had not kept a grip of the local council or the Police, and the club had been raided twice for drugs in the last month alone.

The rumours of the club being used for drugs and prostitution were no longer just rumours. A police raid on the Thursday night had produced all the evidence they needed; cocaine, pills and two girls having full intercourse with a couple of customers in the private dancing booths.

The rumours and the raids all pointed towards the club having its licence revoked. Pete had not mentioned anything about it to him personally, but that was what was bing circulated through the grapevine. He himself was now getting a bad reputation by being associated with the place. Three of his local clients had changed website designer in the last month. Essex was expanding, which he had left to Sara to look after. Kent, which was his market place, was going the other way.

***

Pete put his foot down as he raced his car along the country lanes. Things were not going the way he had expected. He'd thought running a club was going to be easy; easy money, easy birds, a piece of cake, but how wrong could he have been. The club was getting emptier by the week. The weekend clubbers were staying away. There were three other clubs in the town that were doing so much better than his. One club, that had only just opened its doors, was the most popular; you had to pay just to be a member to get in. Pete couldn't even get people in his club with free entry.

With the lack of punters, the drug dealers had even stopped coming. The pole dancing was quiet; girls were not bothering to turn up because there were so few punters, which meant less tips. His boss was not happy, and was now sending down the Hench men. He didn't know what to do, it was one viscous cycle and everything was going against him.

On the other hand, his number one kid, Max was running on a high. He was earning from his web company, the band was doing OK and his band nights were the only time the club had any punters in it. Maybe, he should get Max to run the club.

Pete fought with the steering wheel as he hit a corner too fast, he heard the wheels squeal underneath as they fought to keep a grip on the tarmac, he pushed harder on the accelerator to push the back wheels to gain some grip, clipping the dirt on the edge of the road, he felt the car start to fishtail, lifting off the accelerator and pushing down hard again, he managed to steer out of the corner, and get control just as a huge tree loomed up; he just missed it. Letting out a sigh of relief, he felt his heart beat hard in his chest. "Shit! Fuck it!"" He slowed down a bit and concentrated on the road.

He pulled up onto his driveway and sat in his car for a couple of minutes. He stared down at the Maserati badge on the steering wheel and then looked out at the country cottage he lived in. "Christ! Come on Pete, get a grip, we've been in worst situations than this, we can get out of this shit." He said out loud to himself.

He stepped out the car and made his way to his house. As he opened the front door, he heard soft jazz playing in the living room. He walked in and Olivia was standing by the table lighting candles. "Hey Babe." She smiled.

Pete looked at the table, with the candles and the plates all laid out for dinner, then looked at Olivia, smiling at him. "What the fuck is this?"

Olivia smiled. "I thought it would be nice to have dinner together. I've made some lovely lamb and opened a nice bottle of red."

"Look love, I've had my dinner tonight, I grabbed some in the office." Pete snarled. "I don't want you here making food for me." He made a few strides over to her, grabbed her arm and pulled her to the table. Leaning behind her, close to her ear, he said. "All I want from you is a good fuck when I need it."

"I know Pete." Olivia moaned. "But I thought it would be romantic if we...." She stopped as she heard Pete start to undo his belt.

"Just stick to what you're good at." Pete whispered in her ear. "It has been a shit day."

Chapter 12

Pete sat in his office at the club and waited for the two Hench men to visit. Like him, they had also worked for the boss 'The Governor' since their youth. No one ever called him by his real name. Pete had been with the firm for the last twenty years, starting as a doorman and working his way up to an enforcer, then running a number of enforcers. The club had been part of his expansion plan, so when it had come up for sale, it had been his idea for 'The Governor' to purchase it. He had thought it would be easy running a club. Now he wished he had never seen the 'For Sale' sign.

Olivia, sat on the sofa looking sexy. He had told her to wear something revealing and be nice to everyone today. She had put up a fight and had told him she was not a whore. But she had eventually agreed, after he had promised it would only be for one day and for her troubles he would take her to a nice hotel for the whole weekend; if it all went well. She sat looking worried, fiddling with her nails.

Pete looked at his computer screen again, and looked at the figures, again. There was no way he was going to be able to hide this, he was losing money hand over fist. He had not paid a number of bills to drink suppliers and he was close to having his accounts suspended. He had only just convinced his third supplier to supply on a 'cash-purchase basis' for a couple of grand of spirits, after one of Max's music nights had actually run out of drink. The money they *were* making, was going on staff wages, and when that started costing more than the club was earning, he had no cash to restock his dwindling supply. It was an ever decreasing circle. If he didn't have the drink to sell, he couldn't pay his staff, if he had no staff to serve the drinks he had no income at all.

Pete looked up, as his door was pushed open and in walked The Governor's men. Pete had known them for years; Matt and Derek, both had been with the firm since he had started, both were about ten years older than him and were the trusted men of The Governor; the enforcers of the enforcers.

Matt looked around the office and when his eye caught Olivia on the sofa he suddenly barked. "You, out!" Olivia looked shocked and without even looking at Pete, she got up and left the office like a frighten rabbit.

Pete stayed silent, as the two men sat down, in the chairs opposite his desk. They were not the usual type of men you would expect to be part of 'The Firm', both were dressed in smart handmade suits with highly polished shoes, white shirts and Windsor knotted ties. They both wore gold watches and a matching ring on their pinky-finger of their left hands.

"Hi, Pete." Derek started smiling. "Long-time no see."

"Hi, Derek... Matt." Pete nodded as he smiled back. "Would you like a drink?"

"Double expresso for me, if you do them." Derek answered.

"Yes, we have a machine." Pete explained.

"Water for me Pete." Matt stated. "Sparkling, if you have it." He then added.

Pete got up. "Yes, of course. Give me a couple of minutes and I'll get them sent in." After a minute or so he returned.

"OK, Pete." Derek started. "The Governor has got some concerns about what you're doing here." Pete stayed quiet, he knew that it was not a good idea to start rattling, they knew what they wanted to say and they also knew what outcome they wanted to get. Derek continued. "It was your idea to have this club purchased, and your business plan, to have our money laundered, our drugs sold and a place where our guys could hang out." Derek looked at Pete. "So what has happened?"

"Well...!" Pete paused. "It's not going as I expected, the club had a bad rep before we took it over, that is why it closed in the...."

Derek interjected. "And from what I've heard, you have done nothing to make the reputation any better." Derek paused again. "This was not purchased for you to have your own knocking-shop, this was bought as a business and it is not doing any business...." As Derek was in full flow, Olivia knocked on the door and stepped in. Smiling and flirting, she handed the drinks around, letting her breasts show as she leant forward any chance she got. Pete watched nervously, this was bad timing and now was not a good time to have tits about the place. She left the room. "That's exactly what I'm talking about, Pete. I don't know where you find these birds, but the word is you're playing lord-dick over the women in this place. And that camera up there, is that for security or your little purvey scam?"

Pete could feel his face go a little red. "Come on Derek, that's just a bit of messing about."

"Yeah Pete, just messing about with tarts, but you have a business to run and you are losing our money and The Governor ain't happy. He's ploughed nearly a mil into buying this joint, including the licences, and doing the place up and he ain't happy, and unfortunately for you, it was your idea. So he wants it turned-around or he wants you turned-over."

"Come on, Derek." Pete moaned. "I ain't doing this on purpose, believe me, it's stressing me out. I have all the figures for you here, look, on the computer."

"Shut up." Matt interjected.

Pete looked at Matt, who had said nothing since he had arrived. Out of the two, Matt was the most dangerous. He was a hard man from East London; a big man with a handsome face, but a large body created from all the time he spent in the gym. Those who didn't know him, would take the micky out of his baby face and his small head that was disproportionate to his frame.

"We've been told to come and look at your operation here. You can email the figures to Patrick, who will assess them." Patrick was the firm's accountant, a clever man who never missed a trick and specialised in creative accounting. "We're here to look at how you're running the joint and to look at your staff." He paused. "So, let's go into the bar and have a look at it."

***

They sat at the table in the corner of the restaurant. Matt had just come off his mobile phone. "OK, Pete. I've Just had the word from Patrick." He paused as he looked at Pete's reaction. "From what he sees, from the information you have sent him, you are having fluxes of income." Pete kept quiet. "So, this Max guy, he seems to be the guy that can keep the show on the road. Who is he?"

"He's a young guy, a computer geek. When I first met him, he was still living at home, so I put him up in the pub and set him up in the office next to mine here. He does all our IT and website stuff. He's a loner, he didn't seem to have any hobbies or interest, so I got him to look after one of the bands that played here in the club, just has something to do, and he's taken to it like a fish to water, so I let him have the door."

"You what?" Matt snarled.

"I let him have the door, he used to charge three quid to get in, he now charges a fiver." Pete didn't know where to look. Matt made him feel like a child being chastised.

"Yes and he has, on average, three hundred fucking people in a night! That's fifteen hundred quid. You're lucky to have forty in at a weekend at the moment." Matt sighed.

"Yeah, I know, but that was the deal when we started out." Pete pleaded.

"That deal is going to have to change." Matt snarled.

"If we change it, he won't do it." Pete moaned.

"Well, let me talk to him." Matt snarled. "Where is he?"

"Let me phone him and see if I can't get him to the office this afternoon." Pete picked up his mobile and dialled Max's number.

**

Max walked into the office and was confronted by Pete at his desk and Derek and Matt sitting on the sofa. "Take a seat young man." Matt ordered, Max did as they asked, while he looked worryingly across at Pete, who himself looked anxious.

"What's this all about?" Max asked.

Pete said nothing. Matt spoke first. "Max, is it OK to call you Max?"

Max looked at Matt and then answered. "Yes."

"Hi, Max, I'm Matt and this is my associated Derek." Derek and Max nodded at each other in confirmation.

"Pete here, has got himself into a bit of a pickle." Matt said as he focused between Pete and Max. "This club here, was purchased by The Governor, our boss, and at the moment the club is losing money like it's going out of fashion. Now, The Governor ain't happy about that, and has sent Derek and I down to have a look at what is going on here. Now, as far as we can see, there is nothing untoward that Pete is doing." He looked across at Pete. "Pete here, is just a shit manager." He looked back at Max. "Now, we *know* of some 'tea leafing' going on in the bar and we'll deal with that this evening." Matt smiled. "And, it seems, you run the most successful nights here and take the lion's share of the money, correct?" With that he stopped speaking.

Max said nothing.

Matt smiled again. "Max, we have been talking about you between ourselves, and Pete here speaks very highly of you." Again Matt stopped speaking and Max looked over to Pete who looked a bit worried and again he didn't say anything. "Do you know who we are Max?"

Max looked at the two men and then back at Pete. "No." He stated.

"We work for The Governor and we're called enforcers, do you know what that means Max?"

Max shook his head, he smiled to himself, he couldn't believe this sort of thing actually happened in real life, these guys were trying to put the frighteners on him.

"We make sure that The Governors generosity, is not being abused. The Governor has set up a lot of people in business, and all he wants in return, is his fair share of the cut. Now, here we have Pete, he has a night club, but for some reason no money is coming out of it."

Max looked at Pete and Pete stayed silent in his seat.

"So we are going to stay around for a couple of days, to see what is what and why there is no money being made." Matt looked hard into Max's eyes. "And, I would like to look in your office, so you can show me what you are doing with all those computers.

Max smiled. "Sure."

Matt didn't smile back.

***

Max smiled, as he showed the two goons around his computer systems. They didn't have a clue what he was showing them. He had lost Derek ages ago; he now just wore a vacant glazed look. Matt, had tried to keep up, but he could see that he was struggling. Max laid it on thick, even chucking in some bullshit statements that made no sense to him let alone anyone else.

"So this is all your own business, nothing to do with the club? Why does Pete let you have this office and how much does he charge you for it?" Matt asked.

"Well, Pete charges nothing for the office as I run all this for him." Max tapped on his keyboard and brought up the screens with 'www.Iwilldoanything.com'. There was a young girl on the bed being fucked by some ugly, skinny guy. Max looked at his watch and pulled up another screen on the other monitor. "This screen here, shows all the statements; how many people are logged on, how long they have been on and how much money has been spent, where they are from, etc. Currently we only have five watchers and it's now eleven o'clock."

"Only five? Why so low?" Matt moaned.

"There was a news story on that BBC 'Watchdog' show about internet fraud. Scared a load of punters off." Max stated

"Shit, so this is costing us more than we are earning." Matt stated

"Technically, Yes." Max answered.

"Fucking hell. I've been told that you take the door on this place, and you're earning over a grand a night?" Matt snarled at Max.

Max turned and looked at Matt. "Yes, I am."

"Well, as of now, we are changing that and we are now taking fifty percent of the door." Matt snapped.

Max didn't say anything for a while and then stated. "Well, OK, you can have the door but I won't be putting any band nights on. I'll just go work in another club." Max then added.

"Then I'll kick you out of this office." Matt snapped.

"You kick me out of this office and I will shut the shag-site down." Max stated.

Matt looked at Max. "Look here son, do you know who you're talking to?"

Max smiled. "You've already told me. You're an enforcer."

Matt stared at Max with evil in his eyes. "You best be careful kid, something bad might happen to you."

Max looked at Matt and then at Derek, smiled and then looked back at the computer screen, where the skinny guy was about to cum into the girl's open mouth. Max just raised an eyebrow.

***

Pete stood in his kitchen at home, "Shit Olivia, do something, these boys are getting a bit lively."

"What do you want me to do Pete? You got me wearing this stupid outfit, so that every time I move it practically shows my tits, I might as well be topless. Why are you such a lap dog to these men, and why did you invite them to stay at the house?" Olivia moaned.

"Invite? I didn't fucking invite them to stay, you stupid...! I had no fucking choice!"

Pete looked at her, took another sip of his whisky with his shaky hands. "They work for The Governor and they're checking me out."

"So what? What you got to be worried about?" Olivia asked in a quiet voice.

"I haven't declared the credit card scam, the one that was on the TV the other day." Pete explained, but he didn't know why he even confided in this airhead, she didn't even know what day of the week it was.

"What? That was you?" Olivia looked shocked and then smiled.

"Yes, Olivia! It was fucking me, Oh for fuck's sake!" He shook his head. "They didn't name us, because Mike put the scares on one of the producers, but yes, that was fucking us and I think The Governor knows it was fucking us. He's just trying to find the smoking gun."

"What would they do if they find out?" Olivia asked.

"They will fucking do me over, that's what." Pete looked at Olivia. "I need them distracted, Olivia."

"What do you mean, you need them distracted?"

"For fuck's sake! Look at them, they are getting high of Coke in there and are looking for some action."

"Oh no...no way, not me." Olivia shook her head. "I thought you asked that lady to come round, the one with the band, that housewife you said will do anything."

"Yeah, I have, but she's not fucking here yet is she, she was supposed to be here an hour ago."

"Well, call one of the girls from the club, then." Olivia told him.

"I can't, they'll say I'm abusing company assets for my own fucking use."

Olivia looked at him as he paced up and down the kitchen. "Well, you best hope that that tart turns up then, cos I'm not playing any of your warped games."

Pete grabbed her by the arms. "Well, you may or may not, let's see what fucking happens."

Pete let her go and then turned and walked back into the room to the sound of 'James Brown' on the hi-fi. There was a small mound of cocaine on the table and Matt and Derek both looked at him through slightly glazed eyes. It was only nine o'clock in the evening and the lads looked like they were ready to party.

"Where's the lovely Olivia?" Matt asked. "You are a lucky man Pete, don't know how you get these birds, but she is a babe and those tits..." Pete smiled and shrugged. "Fancy a line?"

Pete looked at the coke and turned the offer down. "Don't do it myself." Just then, Olivia walked into the room.

"Hey! Just in time, fancy a line babe?" Matt asked. She looked at Pete and then at the coke she smiled as she leant down and took a line. Matt watched her naked breasts swaying as she leant down to the glass table to inhale. "Plenty more when you want some babe." Matt smiled.

Olivia sat back in the single chair and relaxed to the sound of the music; she couldn't wait for this night to be over.

Half an hour later there was a knock on the door. Pete jumped up with relief, he went to the door to see Carol standing at the door. "Hi Pete, sorry I'm late, took me an age to get away from the house and it took another age to get Kevin out of the house."

"No worries, you're here now, come in and meet some of my associates." Pete quickly ushered her into the room, and he started to breathe a bit easier. Matt's eyes were already on her. "This is Matt and this is Derek. They are old colleagues from the club business. This is Carol, the mother of the brains behind Yellow Snow; the band Max is looking after."

"Hi, Carol welcome, come and take a seat," Matt tapped the sofa between him and Derek. "I hear your son's band is doing rather well under the guidance of our good friend Max?"

"Yes." Carol looked at Pete then back at Matt. "So, are you here on business or pleasure tonight?" Carol asked.

"They have come down for a visit to see how *business* is going." Pete advised.

"And now, it's the evening, and there is no business to discuss. So let's kick back and have a good time." Matt boomed, the cocaine obviously taking effect on him and changing his mood.

Carol looked at the glass table and then up at Pete. "You want some?" Matt boomed again, smiling he took out a metal tube from his pocket.

"I've never actually tried it." Carol stated, looking nervously at Pete.

"Ah! You'll love it, takes the edge off life, gets you to relax." Matt smiled. "Look, we've had some tonight and it has not harmed us."

Olivia looked at Pete and rolled her eyes. Pete shook his head in a warning not to say anything. In his mind Carol was a big girl and it was her decision, plus the reason she was here was to distract these two buffoons.

"I'm not sure, I've heard a lot of bad things about taking drugs, that once you start you can't stop."

"Rubbish." Matt laughed. "That's just the media, all those fuckers are on it all the time. Give it a go, I'll look after you." Matt winked at Pete. "Look, Olivia's done some tonight, it's not harming her."

"What do you think Pete?" Carol asked, looking at Pete.

"It's your call Carol, but out all the drugs, it's the least addictive, I'm sure one hit won't do you any harm, may give you a good buzz." Pete explained.

Olivia rose from her seat. "Well if you excuse me, I'm off to bed, hope you all have a good time. Night Pete... see you guys in the morning. Nice to meet you Carol." And she walked out the room.

"She's not your usual type Pete, what's up with her?" Matt asked. "Is Carol here more sociable, I wonder?" Rubbing his hand on Carol's knee.

Carol turned to look at Pete and then to the cocaine on the table. "Go on Carol, just one try and see what you think."

"OK, just one try." She smiled.

"You only regret the things you don't do." Matt cut a line for her with a razor blade and then passed her the metal tube. "Just put that to your nose and snort it back."

Carol leant forward on her knees and snorted the line, she then sat back and let the light headiness hit her, she smiled as she looked at Pete.

***

Max sat with Angela and he watched her push her food around her plate, she hadn't said anything since she had met him that night.

"What is it?" He asked, "You haven't said much all night."

She looked up from her plate, "Max it's you and the people you're mixed up with."

"What?" He exclaimed. "What are you talking about, what people?"

"The people from the club." She looked sad. "People have been talking, they have said some bad things about the club, the people, about YOU!"

"What people, what are you talking about?" Max asked.

"At my work, the news people, they're ridiculing me behind my back, call me a gangster's mole, asking me where I can get some gear and all that." Her face turned sharp. "Are you involved with pornography?" She stared at him. "And don't lie to me."

"It's not what you think!" He exclaimed. "I...." She dropped her cutlery causing her knife to fall against her plate and bounce onto the floor and she stood up.

"So it *is* true." She snarled. "You bastard."

Max looked around the restaurant, it seemed everyone had stopped eating and now focussed on his table; he felt small. He tried to calm Angela down. "Please Angela, calm down. Sit back…"

"Oh, just fuck off." She said, just a bit too loud for is liking, and stormed off. He tried to catch her and grab her arm, but she was too quick and was already half way across the room.

"Excuse me, Sir, the bill?" One of the waiters called out as Max raced through the restaurant entrance.

"Give me a minute, I'll be back to pay." Max said sharply as the door closed behind him. He chased Angela up the pathway and as he got close he put his hand on her shoulder to try and stop her but she shrugged it off. "Come on Angela, it's not what you think. It's all about the money. It pays a fortune."

Angela stopped, turned and glared at Max. "You are taking advantage of people for your own wealth. You are using people."

"No, I'm not. I have no dealings with these people whatsoever. I just provide a service and that's it."

"It's wrong Max, and if you can't see that then I have nothing more to say to you." She turned and stormed off as Max stood and watch her leave.

"Well it's all right for you! I've had to earn all the money I make. It's easy to take the moral high ground when you've money given to you on a plate!" Max screamed after her.

"Fuck off Max, and crawl back into the sewer you crawled out of." He heard her shout without turning.

Max turned and walked back to the restaurant, paid the bill for a meal they hadn't even eaten and went home.

***

Carol was swaying to the beat of the music in the middle of the room with a glass of wine in her hand. Matt and Derek sat on the sofa smiling at her, enjoying the show. Pete turned to them "Right then chaps, that's me done, I'm off to bed now, you know where your rooms are, see you in the morning."

"Yeah, OK Pete, see you in the morning." Derek answered, Matt said nothing, his attention stayed on Carol.

Pete went to his bathroom, brushed his teeth, washed his face and then made his way to his bed. Olivia was lying there watching the TV. "What you watching?"

"Nothing really, there's a film on but I'm not really watching it." Pete climbed into the bed and pulled the cover down off her exposing her breasts. He moved up close to her and cupped a breast. "Pete, I'm not really in the mood."

Pete just forced her onto her front and put his weight on her. "But I am." He snarled.

"Pete, what is wrong with you, I don't want this." Olivia moaned.

"You're in my house, in my bed and you will do what I tell you." He pushed his knee between her legs to open her up.

"Pete! I don't want to." Olivia tried to move away, but struggled against his weight. She felt his hard penis pressed against her bum. "Get off me!"

Pete pushed himself into her. "Take it and love it baby…."

***

"Show us some skin Carol." Matt sneered from where he was sitting, "You are an attractive lady and I love the shapes you're making baby." Carol smiled, waved her finger at him, she kept swaying to the music. "Come on babe, it's only us here, let's have some fun."

Derek stood up and made his way to the drinks cabinet swaying to the music with a smile on his face. He turned and looked at Carol.

"Do you fancy another line babe?" Carol smiled and nodded.

"Well, now, you're going to have to show us some skin if you want some more." Carol teased him and again waved her finger.

"Well, there's no Charlie for you then." Derek pulled a small packet from his pocket and moved over to the glass coffee table and poured out a small amount of white powder, with his blade he started to organise the powder into six lines.

Matt jumped up, snorted two and then returned back to the sofa. Derek snorted two, then turned to Carol. "There are two lines for you, if you want them?" Carol looked down at the drug and made a move to come over. "But you are going to have to show us some skin."

Carol shrugged and smiled and as she swayed over to the table, she started to undo her buttons on her blouse. Matt smiled. "You are a fit lass, love." She removed her blouse slowly. "Now get those tits out babe." Matts face beamed with excitement. Carol removed her bra and went to move to the coffee table. "Skirt as well babe." She paused and looked at the two men; they were not what she would call handsome, neither of them were her type, but what the hell, they were Pete's friends and Pete was helping her son get to where he wanted to be. She stood, lowered her skirt zip and let it fall to the ground. She now stood in her black thong and her high heeled shoes. She felt all empowering and she liked it.

"*Now*, you can have your lines, you, sexy little minx." Derek smiled and passed Carol the metal tube. She bent over the table and took a line. Derek cupped one of her breasts as she leant over to snort the second. She then sat back on her knees, unpinned her hair so it fell to her shoulders and looked at the two men and wiped the residue from her nose.

"So, which of us do you want to try first?" Derek asked.

"Why don't you both try me at the same time." Carol smiled.

***

Pete rolled Olivia onto her front when he had finished, his sweat dripping down upon her. He snarled at her as he raised himself to his knees and punched her hard in the stomach. He then punched her again and again. Oliva couldn't shout as the wind had been knocked out of her on the second punch. "That is it, bitch, I've had enough of you and your prissy fucking ways. You do what I fucking tell you or I'll fucking kill you." Pete screamed at her. He then leant over to the side of the bed and pulled out a pair of handcuffs from the draw, attached one end to her wrists and the other to the bedpost. He rolled onto his back and fell asleep. Olivia whimpered at his side.

Chapter 13

"Morning Guys, how did you get on last night?" Pete smiled.

Both men were sitting around the kitchen table with mugs of coffee. "Great, nothing was off limits with that one, she was up for anything. Wanna see?" Derek went to pick up his phone from the table.

"No thanks, you're alright." Pete laughed. "I'm surprised she let you film her though, being married and all that."

"She was totally out of it, by the time we filmed this." Derek smiled and Matt nodded with a grin.

"Is she still here then?" Pete asked.

"Nah, she left with her tail between her legs around five this morning, cursing and swearing as if she had somewhere else to be." Both Matt and Derek laughed. "Well, where's breakfast then man, a man can't do a day's work without his breakfast." Derek groaned.

"And breakfast will be provided." Pete said as Olivia entered the room wearing nothing but a baby-doll nightie. Both men around the table looked at her slightly wide mouthed. "Now that's more like it Pete." Matt commented. "Last night I had this one done as a cold fish."

"Yeah, well, we've had a little chat and she's going to be a bit more appreciative of her surroundings from now on." Pete announced.

Olivia took the orders for two full English and to Pete's surprise was rather adapt in the kitchen and came up with a perfect breakfast. Olivia herself only had a slice of toast.

Derek and Matt tucked in and said nothing until Derek mopped up the last bit of baked bean sauce with the last of the bread and said. "Now that was lovely babes." He smiled, burped and looked Olivia up and down. "Now love, before we start talking business with your fella here, come over here and let me show my appreciation for such lovely service."

A sadistic smile covered Pete's face as he nodded to Olivia. "Now sit down love, sit on my knee, like a good little girl." Stone cold, Olivia did as she was told. Derek grabbed her breasts and sighed, "These are so nice, so young and so full." He then took Olivia hands and pulled them towards the zipper on his trousers. "I've brought you a present, why don't you undo my trousers and see what's inside." Olivia winced but played along. "It's something for you to sit on, you do want to sit on it don't you Olivia?" Olivia said nothing, until she heard Pete. "Answer him Olivia, don't be so rude, you were brought up better than that weren't you."

"Well, sweetheart?"

"Yes, I do." Olivia begrudgingly answered.

"That's it then, on you get, I've been wanting to do this to you, since I stepped through the door yesterday.

***

Matt stood behind Olivia and turned to Derek. "While you're filling your boots, I'll have a chat with Pete. But don't you go anywhere Olivia, I want a go after him."

Matt turned to Pete. "Let's leave them in peace and go through to the other room."

Pete followed Matt into the living room, Matt suddenly turned on Pete and grabbed him around the neck. "Look, you dozy fat cunt. I know what you are up to with that faggot Max." He snarled inches from Pete's face. "Don't think you can lay on some slags for us and a couple of beers and we'll just potter back to The Governor and tell him all is hunky fucking dory down here."

"Matt, what you talking about?" Pete choked through the neck hold. "What do you mean?"

Matt grabbed Pete's crouch with his other hand and squeezed hard. Pete's squealed and began to curl, but Matt kept him standing with his strangle hold. "I'm not your average cunt Pete. I'm happy to fuck your whores, drink your booze, but if you're creaming off the top, I want my cut. Fuck Derek, in there with his dick up her fanny. Fuck The Governor, he hasn't got long left, the Turks are taking over anyway and his time is running out. I want out, and I plan to be off to Spain on my boat before too long. So, Pete, the web shit, and the credit card scams, that you don't think I know about, I want my cut and I want it quickly. £500K by the end of the week and this stays between us. I want it in euro's and carried to a French Bank Account in Paris."

"Matt, I can't, how can I get that sorted in a week?" Pete begged.

"Don't take me for a fucking mug Pete, I can see how much you and the geek are lifting. There's been no cash flow up the chain from those sites and after visiting nerd-boy's office, his screen clearly showed how many users were on the site, it also showed some mean-figures that Maxy-boy didn't expect me to understand. A little bit of arithmetic, even in my pinhead, gives you a bigger turnover than what is being filtered up. Plus, the scamming you have going on, on the side, I doubt The Governor even knows about that bit!"

"Matt, it's not as you think. Since 'Watchdog', the credit card stuff really fell away."

"Bollocks! I want that money, I'll be watching your webcam site at exactly 10pm next Friday, the minute I see that slag in there, shagging two black men, I'll see it as a sign that you have done your bit. So best you get everything sorted by then." Matt dropped Pete's balls and he fell to the floor. "Now let's go and see if Olivia is in the mood for another present, as this chat has just given me a nice boner."

Chapter 14

Pete was speaking over the hands-free system in his car, with Olivia in the passenger seat. She was now slightly dazed from the pills he had given her to calm her down. Matt and Derek had been pawing her most of the morning. He had frantically tried to reach Max with no luck. He had called Mike and put the word out to find him urgently. He needed as many credit cards as possible and pull in the £500K. There was no way he wanted any trouble from Matt or The Governor.

Mike spoke through the speakers. "Pete, bad news, Max seems to have disappeared, he's not been in his office for a few days, I broke in there this morning and have been going through the site and have managed to lift fifty cards."

"Fifty! For fuck's sake, you'll be lucky to get a grand on each. Fuck it! Find him." Pete snarled as he thumped the steering wheel with both hands.

"We're trying, he's not in the pub, we don't know where he is." Mike pleaded through the speakers.

"Try fucking harder! Try his mums and that slag housewife who works for him. Someone knows where the cunt is." Pete paused. "Also, get a hold of that film director; I need three black animals for ten o'clock Friday night. Tell them they have a nice little blonde to ruin. No holds barred."

"OK Pete, let me sort it and I'll send some lads out to see if we can find Max."

"Thanks, Mike." Pete pressed the button on his steering wheel to hang up. He gunned the car and accelerated towards Maidstone racking his brains along the way. '£500K, fucking £500K!' He had squirreled a load of the money away, but £500K was going to leave him well short for his own exit plan.

Olivia's head rolled in the sports seat as they cornered at speed. Not the way he wanted to break this one, but it was now well out of his hands. Now she was doped up, that was the way she was going to stay, until Friday night anyway. He looked over at her; 'God knows where she'd end up after that.' He thought.

Max woke with Angela cuddled up to his chest. He stared at the ceiling and then looked around the room. He was in her flat, a new build on the edge of the river Medway. They had sat on the balcony last night with a bottle of wine, watching the traffic pass, watching the young people enjoying a night out. A few boats had moored with people boarding to enjoy the warm evening weather, while other boats gentle passed up and down.

He had managed to convince her that he was out of the scene with Pete, he was off-loading the band and dropping the websites. He was going to take his money, and just concentrate on share dealing, until he worked out his next move. Maybe he would go into the film business, Angela knew her way around, maybe he would become a producer, be the money man. The world was his oyster, he just needed a new plan.

The first day, of the rest of his new life, started with the beautiful view of his girlfriend's half naked body, he smiled and asked if she wanted a cup of tea. Angela half opened one eye, shook her and put her head back on the pillow. Max quietly closed door behind him and made his way across the open plan lounge to the kitchen area. His phone was vibrating on the coffee table, but he ignored it. He made a coffee with the fancy looking Nespresso machine and made his way to the balcony, picking his phone up as went; eighteen missed calls, and twelve text messages. He stared at the phone and then started to read the text, each one becoming more threatening as he made his way through. He was tempted to just put the phone down and ignore the lot, but decided to make a call to Pete. The phone rang twice before it was answered with a short.

"Where the fuck, *are* you Max?"

"Why? What's with all the calls and text messages. You do know I don't work for you anymore."

"Look you little shit, where are you?"

"Maidstone."

"Well, get over to the club right now, I want a chat." Max could picture the snarl of Pete face through the phone.

"OK Pete, I'll come over, but for fuck sake calm down. Give me twenty minutes."

***

As Max walked into Pete's office, he was greeted by a stressed Pete pacing behind his desk, and a doped-up Olivia slumped on the sofa with a blank face nursing a mug of tea; she didn't smile or even acknowledge Max as he entered.

"Sit, Max, sit, why have you not been answering your phone?" Pete barked.

"Look Pete, you're not my boss, and I don't live by my phone. What's so important that you need me here asap?"

"How much money we got in the web account? I need three hundred taken out by the end of the week and turned into cash." Pete rapidly told Max.

"What? Why?" Max asked.

"Don't worry about why, have we got it?" Pete sort of pleaded.

"Yeah, we've got it, but we need it to pay for the site, the girls and the crew. We could probably release £250K, this week."

"I need the full £300K."

"Hang on, you need? And what about my cut? Fifty percent of the profits are mine, so that's £125K you can have."

Pete stood and slammed his fist on the desk. "I need the fucking £300K so give it to me. You are coming to the bank and we're going to withdraw the funds."

"And how the fuck, are you going to pay me back? This sounds like a shut and run Pete."

"Look, Max, I need to pay someone off before they have my bollocks. Once I have the money, you take the site and the operation, it's all yours."

"I don't want it, I was going to come and see you and pass it all over to you. Take my cut and call it quits."

"Well, you can't, I need it! Now I'm going to call the bank and tell them we are pulling the money from the account."

***

Matt sat on the sofa with a naked girl lying next to him, she looked no older than fourteen, now that her red lipstick and fake eyelashes were missing. He had met her sitting at the bar, in Pete's club after popping in to try and find him. She had accepted his offer of a drink, and some blow; in exchange for blowing-him-off in the toilet. He had had some time to kill, and had ordered a bottle of bubbly from the barman, who was told in no uncertain terms, to put it on the house. He had only drunk one glass, the rest had been polished off, along with five lines of cocaine, by his new found, pretty little nympho. He had given her a good feel-up in the toilets, but had waited until he got her back to his hotel room before his perverted fun started.

"What are you looking at?" She slurred, as Matt opened his laptop and logged onto 'www.Iwilldoanything.com'. He looked at the clock; it was five to ten.
The girl sat next to him, puzzled as they looked at the screen of an empty bed. "Don't you like me anymore?" She slurred as she ran her hand up his inner thigh.

"In a minute, I've just got to check something. Do you want another line?" The girl nodded. Matt took a foil wrap out of his pocket and emptied it out on the table, with his razor blade from his glasses case, he cut the powder into four lines.
"What you carrying that blade for?" The girl asked.

"None of your worries lover." From the same case he took his metal snorting pipe.

"Hey babe, do you want me to blow some of this in your arse? Gives you a good rush." Matt asked.

"I've never tried that, I don't know, I've never done anything with my arse before."

Matt just grinned, 'Oh, thank you Lord, a lovely little arse virgin,' he thought. "Let me watch this sweetheart, and then I'll sort you out."

He watched the screen, and saw Olivia appear and climb onto the bed, she looked high and pissed, her eyes glazed, her lips glistened red with smudged high gloss lipstick, she wore a dress that revealed her cleavage and just about covered her arse, she wore shocking pink high heels and glistening stockings.

Someone was in the room talking to her, giving her instructions. She looked at the camera and then focused on something. Matt typed on this laptop. 'Blow me a kiss Beautiful.' He saw Olivia's eyes focus and then she smiled, giggled and blew a kiss.

Matt then typed 'Show me that peachy arse' Olivia smiled and then turned from the camera and on her hands and knees pulled her skirt up to show her thong. She wiggled a bit and Matt felt his cock harden.

"Hey, love come here." He turned to the girl on his bed. "I want you to suck me off." The young girl him looked at him, then at the lines of cocaine and the bottles of champagne on the table, smiled and came and knelt in front of him, undid his trousers and pull his hard penis out and started to suck him off.

Matt typed again. 'Now take that dress off and show me those tits.' Matt typed into the keyboard. Olivia obeyed and this excited him further. He had already fucked this girl for real, but with her on the end of the keyboard, doing exactly what she was told, seemed even more erotic to him.

He could feel himself building up while the girl sucked him. He used his elbow to keep her head on his cock while he watched Olivia strip. 'Do you like black cock?' He typed. Olivia smiled and nodded. 'Do you want a black cock?' Olivia giggled and nodded again. Suddenly her face went white and her eyes bulged, as three large, naked black men bounded into the room. Matt smiled.

'Oh, fuck me!' Pete had excelled himself; three, he had only asked for two, this obviously meant he was definitely going to get the money.

He watched the screen, and saw Olivia get pinned to the bed by one of the men and his large, thick, black cock pushed into her face, another pulled her legs wide apart and before the third guy got to the bed, he had cum into the girl's mouth, she tried to pull away but he held her there with his elbow waiting for her to stop struggling and swallow his cum.

The girl lifted her head and smiled. "Did I do good?"
"Yeah, yeah babe, now get on the bed and get on your hands and knees." He stood and undressed completely, he scooped up the cocaine from the table, grabbed his metal pipe and positioned her, so he could still see the TV.

"Now Babe, show me that arse and hold it apart." He climbed on the bed and slapped her backside. She giggled and then with no inhibitions, she pulled her arse apart for him. Matt took some cocaine into the pipe, inserted it into her and blew. He slapped her arse again, he was hard, he spat on her, inserted a finger and made her moan. When he felt her muscle relax, he knelt behind her and inserted himself slowly, when he was fully in, he started to fuck her. She cried out in pain and he pushed her head into a pillow.

Chapter 15

Pete sat in his room, on his own, with the money in a briefcase sitting under his desk. Matt was due at any time. He had not heard from Carol, since the party night with Matt and Derek, and she had not returned any of his calls. He was tempted to go round to her house, but he didn't want to chance running into her husband.

Max had not been seen either, since he had handed over the £300K. The website was still running; The Governor had now taken it over with his own team. Max had handed over all the passwords and access codes without even blinking and eyelid. At the time he was pleased to be shot of it.

Max had then disappeared; he had no idea where he was. He had thought he might have been with Yellow Snow, but they seemed to have someone else looking after them now, a 'roady' of some sorts. He knew they were in London tonight, on some big-gig and were on the verge of signing for Warner Brothers.

'Fuck it!' He thought, this had all got a bit fucking messy. Why he ever thought he could run a night club was beyond him. He had only thought about the perks; easy access to women, booze, and a nice bit of the kickbacks. Everything had gone wrong, the club had failed, the drugs had not sold, and he had come under the attention of The Governor. If he hadn't, he could have just kept going, taking the small kickbacks and feeding the acceptable amount up the food chain.

But instead, here he was with £500k slipping out of his hands and going to someone who was about to run. He had a further £200K or so stashed, but that wasn't going to get him far. He was going to have to skip, and skipping over to Spain was not going to be an option; too many people would know him, or of him, and would hand him back. He was going to have to go off-piste, Greece, he loved Greece. USA was out, as they wouldn't let him in with his criminal record and drug offences.

The door suddenly opened, and in strolled Matt all smiles. Dressed in a light suit with brown shoes, looking as far from being 'hired-help' as could be. You could have mistaken him for a ranch-farmer or an ex-pat in some foreign country.

"So where's Derek?" Pete asked.
"Don't you worry about Derek; he's been held up entertaining."
"So, you planning to be off, then, this is it?" Pete asked. "You look like you're about to go off on your holidays."
"That's the plan, Pete. I am indeed off on my holidays; sunny Spain. Marbella if you want to know."

"Not really, but there you go." Pete stated. "What's The Governor going to do when he knows you have skipped town?"

"I'll be surprised if he's even around in the next 24 hours. The Turks want his territory and he's a bit too old, hasn't moved with the times. I know he's going, as I've got my ear to the streets and I know the lay of the land."

"Nothing that you may have helped arrange then?" Pete looked up at Matt.

"Well, you're cleverer than you look Peter, so you have noticed the 'Turks' around here in the last few weeks? Checking you out, checking your security, you've noticed that there's been no dealers in the club? They were warned off weeks ago. They'll be in sooner than later, to take over."

"So what are you doing then Matt, if you knew all about this, what are you doing? You've been with the firm boy to man, you ran errands at the age of thirteen, like the rest of us."

"Times change, we grow up, and now it's time to get out, go legit. I'm off to the med I've set up a boat charter service and it's all ready to go." Matt smiled. "And now I need to go, so where's my money?"

"It's all here, under my desk." As his eyes looked down and the words left Pete's mouth, the door behind Matt, swung open and Mike rushed through welding a crow bar above his head and in one fast, forceful downward drive, he drove it into the back of Matt's skull; Matt's legs buckled and he fell to the floor.

Pete looked at Mike. "Fucking well done Mike. Shit., right, now come on, let's get rid of the body." He pulled and envelope from his draw and threw it at Mike. "There's hundred kay in there. Once you've dumped the body, I suggest you get whatever other money you have, and get as far away from this shit as you can. Take it to the warehouse like we discussed, no one will find it there or even think to look anywhere near that place."

Mike nodded, as Pete picked up his briefcase, he looked around the office one last time, slapped Mike on the back and said. "Gods Speed."

***

Pete put his briefcase behind the driver's seat of his Maserati, got in and floored it towards the M20 and the Eurotunnel terminal.

***

Max sat on the balcony with Angela, with his feet up drinking a cold beer. He was staring out at pleasure boats pass on the Medway.
"I love boats, don't you Angela?"
"Not really, I get sea sick."
"Shame..."
"So, what do you plan to do now?" Angela asked.
"What I originally planned, play the stock market. I can be anywhere in the world to do that."
"What about the web company and your clients? They have businesses to run, you can't just leave them in the lurch." Angela asked.

"No Angela, you don't know me at all do you, I'm not into destroying peoples' businesses, far from it. I've already handed over all the company details to Sara. She can do what she wants with it. She's been doing a good job in her area, while I've been messing about with this shit."

"So that's it then, you are going to just walk away from it all?"

"Yep!"

"But will they let you?"

"Well, from what Pete's saying, this is probably the best time to do a split. He said there's about to be a coup, and it looks like this will be a decisive and aggressive takeover. They will not miss us; I have already handed over all the bits of mine that they could have interest in.

The whole thing was organised on separate servers, servers in Seattle for the content on 'Idoanything.com' and 'Your Web Page Design' are in Canary Wharf through different accounts so there is connection to her."

"They won't miss us?"

"What?"

"You said…They won't miss *us*?" She looked suspiciously at him.

"What, what you talking about I meant me. They won't miss me!"

"So that's it then you just sail away into the sunset?"

"Yep, I'm meeting up with a friend who's thinking of setting up a new boat chartering business. So, yes I might just sail away into the sunset!"

'Sail all the way to Greece. I love Greece.' Max thought as his eyes smiled.'

The End

Find John Marsh on Facebook & Twitter for updates and information.

If you liked this book you will enjoy these other titles by Percy Publishing

Hearts of Green by John Marsh

https://www.amazon.co.uk/Hearts-Green-John-Marsh/dp/0957156820/ref=sr_1_1?ie=UTF8&qid=1485694859&sr=8-1&keywords=hearts+of+green+by+john+marsh

This Time Round by Ray Quinn

https://www.amazon.co.uk/d/Books/Time-Round-Ray-Quinn/0992929873/ref=sr_1_1?ie=UTF8&qid=1485695223&sr=8-1&keywords=this+time+round+by+ray+quinn